CLARKESWORLD

8

FICTION

NON-FICTION

Neil Clarke: Publisher/Editor-in-Chief
Sean Wallace: Editor
Kate Baker: Non-Fiction Editor/Podcast Director

Clarkesworld Magazine (ISSN: 1937-7843) • Issue 218 • November 2024

clarkesworldmagazine.com

LuvHome™

RESA NELSON

Naked except for her pink fluffy robe and slip-on shoes, Dyna stumbled when her own front door shoved her out into the condo building's fourth-floor hallway. As the door's lock clicked shut, Dyna realized her home had deceived her.

She slammed her palm against the rigid door, instantly regretting the sharp sting that rattled every bone in her hand. Shaking it as if to get rid of the pain, Dyna shouted at the door. "What is wrong with you?"

The oval displaying 414—the number of her condo unit—rolled back to display a small speaker. "Not a thing, Luv," her condo said in a male British voice that leaned toward a Cockney accent. "Just doing what's best."

Ten minutes ago, Dyna had come awake and shrugged when she noticed the time had passed mid-morning. In her younger days, she'd loved being an early riser, typically waking up at sunrise, anxious to get an early start.

But those days were long gone.

Thank goodness she'd tugged on her fluffy pink bathrobe this morning—wait, now it all made sense.

The shock of the bedroom floor's cold surface after her feet left the cozy bedclothes.

The slip-on shoes she couldn't remember leaving next to her bed. The LuvHome™ must have placed them there while she slept.

Her own home had set her up.

Dyna tugged on the edge of her bathrobe caught in the door, which now held her captive in the hallway, naked except for the bathrobe and shoes. Fuming, she shouted, "I'm the one in charge. I'm the one who activated you. Your job is to do what I say."

“That’s what I’m doing.” Her new home’s voice paused as if considering infinite variables. “More or less.”

“Let me back in!”

“You can’t shut out the world and hide from it,” the British voice said in a bright and friendly tone. “It ain’t good for you.”

Infuriated, Dyna gave up on the trapped bathrobe and pounded a fist against the door. “I’m stuck. I can’t go anywhere because you’re malfunctioning.” She pounded her fist until it ached. “Let me loose, you can of sardines.”

Before she realized what happened, the door cracked open and the edge of her bathrobe fell free.

“There you go, Luv. Free to go anywhere you want.” Brightness fell from the voice. “And there’s no need to get snippy. All I’m doing is what’s right.”

The temperature in the hallway plummeted.

Dyna shivered. “What’s going on?”

“Already spelled it out, nice and proper in the paperwork you signed when you bought me. But to get more specific, you need to get out and meet people. Eat food that’s good for you. And get some exercise. You’ve done yourself no good by lying around all day doing nothing but eating junk. That’s all you’ve done ever since moving in. I’ve had a chat with the places that deliver your takeout meals, and they’ve agreed to ignore your future orders. I’ve told them what to send instead.”

Dumbfounded, Dyna sputtered some choice obscenities before saying, “You have no right to do that! You’re my home. You have to do what I say.”

“I’ll have a nice cup of tea waiting for you when you get back.” The oval with her unit number rolled over to cover the speaker, a clear indication that her home had terminated the conversation.

Dyna shouted and kicked the door to no avail. For the first time, she appreciated the chip implant that had been required when she purchased her LuvHome™ last month. She whispered into her thumb. “Call LuvHome™ property management.” She’d show her stupid home. She’d report it and get someone out here to pry the door open with a crowbar, if need be.

Small blue letters glowed through her skin. “Blocked.”

Blocked? Since when?

Dyna’s eyebrows furrowed in rage.

The word faded from her skin, replaced by the words: “Exit now.”

Dyna stomped down the hallway toward the elevator. But when she pushed the Down button, a pleasant female voice said, “Elevator temporarily out of order. Please use the stairs instead.”

Still boiling with fury, Dyna spoke through clenched teeth. "I can wait."

"Stairs are highly recommended. There is currently no repair scheduled for this elevator."

Dyna looked pointedly at three elevators standing side by side. "Then let me use one that's working."

"Apologies. All three elevators are out of order." A glowing green arrow appeared on the wall between two of the elevators. "If you are not already familiar with the stairs, simply follow the arrows to find them."

Dyna mustered every ounce of willpower to keep from shrieking as she continued down the hallway and stomped down four flights of stairs.

Located downtown in a small city, Dyna had bought this condo because of its proximity to everything, even though she'd never ventured outside since moving in. The commuter rail and bus station required a two-block walk. Museums, restaurants, shops, and small gardens stood within a one-mile radius.

Now standing alone in her building's lobby, Dyna peeked through the enormous windows facing the main street.

Surprisingly, no one peeked back, each pedestrian and driver and passenger too absorbed in his or her OwnWorld™.

Dyna schemed until she thought of a way to defeat her condo and figure out a way to get back inside. Once that happened, she'd never leave again.

Not ever.

Dyna remembered a cute little clothing shop a few blocks away. Mindful to not draw attention to herself, she eased out of the building and glided along those few blocks, successful at staying invisible by not drawing attention to herself. When she entered the clothing shop, Dyna started at the sound of a tinkling bell on the door.

An android with a screen face approached and said, "Is there something I can help you find?"

Dyna scrunched her nose in distaste. "I don't suppose you have any real humans working here."

"Oh." The android removed its screen face to reveal a human one. It wasn't an android, after all. "I'm Katy," said the young woman now holding the screen face in one hand. "Sorry about the android appearance. The tourists get a kick out of them, and I hate to disappoint."

Dyna had decided to move to this small city because of its popularity as a tourist destination, which meant lots of museums and high-quality restaurants for the locals to enjoy, not to mention the weekly farmers market.

Katy waved away the pretty dresses designed for the younger crowd and led Dyna to the consignment racks. She discovered a nice pair of jeans and a lightweight cardigan/sweater set. She changed into them, and Katy presented a big paper bag for the fluffy pink bathrobe Dyna had worn into the shop.

At checkout, Dyna rambled. "I hope the payment works. My chip has been acting up today."

But as Dyna stepped onto the scanner threshold, the chip embedded in the fleshy part of her thumb gave a happy beep. The word "Paid" flashed in green letters through her skin.

As a pair of tourists entered the shop, Katy hurriedly put her screen mask back on and called out to Dyna, "Come back any time!"

Relieved to be fully dressed and decent, Dyna checked a huge city map displayed on the sidewalk for tourists and then marched at a steady and determined pace toward the local police station. After announcing her request to an IntelligentAssistant™ at the front desk, she fidgeted in a chair in the station's empty foyer until a middle-aged uniformed man beckoned for her to follow him into a nearby office.

The police officer sat behind a small desk and tapped on its surface. He studied the graphics it displayed. Without looking at Dyna, he said, "You're here about a break-in?"

"No!" Dyna said in astonishment. "My home ejected me. It won't let me back in."

The officer's shoulders sagged, and he ran his hands over his face as if trying to stay awake. "You mean your husband locked you out?"

"No!" Dyna insisted. "I live downtown at LuvHomes™. My home is supposed to . . . "

Love me.

"My home is supposed to take care of me," Dyna continued. "But it's gone crazy. Something in my home has misfired. Its wires are crossed. I need help getting back inside my own home."

Finally, the officer looked up, his face edged with irritation. "I thought those places couldn't do anything without your permission."

"Exactly!" Dyna sat back in her chair with crossed arms, grateful the officer understood.

"You have a chip?"

Dyna raised a hand, and her thumb blushed pink.

"Place your hand here, please." The officer pointed at the center of the desk's surface.

When Dyna did so, her thumb beeped repeatedly and then made a grinding noise, as if she'd removed the chip from her thumb and dropped the chip into a garbage disposal. She jerked her hand back and cradled it against her chest.

The officer studied the newly displayed graphics for a few minutes. Pointing at them, he said, "Here's your problem. You bought what they're calling a 'best solution' option. As far as I can make out, you agreed to let your home decide what's best for you."

Indignant, Dyna said, "I did no such thing."

But secretly she wondered if maybe she'd made a mistake. Maybe she had selected that option without realizing what it meant. Or maybe she'd been distracted. She couldn't remember choosing the "best solution" option, but she couldn't remember not choosing it either.

The graphics pinged repeatedly, and a red-and-white bullseye displayed on top of them.

"Go ahead," the police officer said to the pinging bullseye.

"We acknowledge that Dyna Wilson has accessed her own records," said a pleasant female voice with a Bermuda accent. "Please inform her that she is her own problem. She will be allowed back inside her home when she learns how to get out of her own way."

Dyna recoiled in horror.

"Well," the police officer said with a shrug. "That's that." He swept his hand across the desktop to clear all images.

"That's that?" Dyna said. "I thought you were the police. I thought you were supposed to help people. And all you can say is 'that's that?'"

The police officer gave her an unrelenting gaze. "M'am. No law has been broken. And you appear to be unharmed."

Dyna bit back her frustration. "But I can't get back inside my own home!"

The officer stood and gestured toward the door.

Dragging herself away from the police station, a wave of weakness overwhelmed Dyna. She glanced up at the midday sun and realized she'd had nothing to eat since rolling out of bed this morning. Light-headed, she walked past every popular restaurant boasting a waitstaff of drones and robots until she spotted a small diner.

Dyna minced her way inside the diner. Before she could change her mind and leave, a real human waitress popped into view and seated her at a booth. Dyna placed the paper bag containing her bathrobe on the red leather seat next to her.

A short time later, a strong cup of coffee and a cheddar-and-spinach omelet gave her focus and resolve.

Why should she let her own home boss her around? Dyna knew who she was and what she wanted. She was the one who knew best for herself, not some ridiculous AI.

After finishing her breakfast and paying for it, Dyna stormed the few blocks back to her building, ready to convince her own front door to open and let her back inside.

But when she tried to enter the building, its glass doors clicked shut, even though she knew the lobby doors were supposed to be open at all hours.

"Hey!" Dyna shouted at the lobby. "I need to get in. I live here!"

The building refused to respond. It ignored her.

Dyna tried hiding behind a column near the building's entrance with the hope that a resident or delivery person would cause the doors to open and that she could dash in behind them. But despite a decent amount of foot traffic on the sidewalk, no one tried to enter the building.

If not for the dang chip in her thumb, she might have tried cobbling together some type of disguise. Dyna knew that even if she pretended to be someone else, the building would recognize the chip. She had no way to fool the building into letting her enter.

Dyna saw only one possibility.

She would play along. She would do whatever her home wanted and pretend to be on board.

But once Dyna wrangled her way back inside, she would never go outside again.

"Fine," Dyna said to the building, hoping she sounded agreeable. "What do you want me to do?"

Following each arrow displayed on her thumb, Dyna took an easy walk to the Downtown Y, where she immediately encountered an old-model TrueReceptionist™ at the front desk, flanked by half-doors allowing members in and out of the Y—and keeping non-members out.

The receptionist existed as little more than a screen on top of a cylinder mounted on the counter, which allowed the receptionist's face to spin 360 degrees, like a possessed child from an ancient movie. The receptionist made loud clunking noises as it turned to face Dyna. When it spoke, the receptionist's voice went up and down like an out-of-control roller coaster. "Oh, Ms. Wilson. You have arrived at last!"

Dyna glanced down at her thumb, which now blinked green. "I don't know what I'm doing here. I never signed up for a membership."

"No worries!" The receptionist's screen spun in circles and then came to a screeching stop, facing the wall behind it. It slowly cranked back to face Dyna, all the while sounding like its bolts were coming loose. "Your home bought a ten-year membership for you. It told me you were once a competitive swimmer, so I've taken the liberty of printing a swimsuit, flip flops, and a towel for you. You'll find them in the ladies changing room by Locker 112."

The screen increased its brightness level, as if beaming with pride.

The half-door marked "Entrance" swung open. The floor displayed arrows that created a path.

"OK," Dyna said with trepidation. She walked past the receptionist. "Thanks."

At Locker 112, Dyna discovered a racer-back suit with a pattern of blue and white bubbles. She liked it, even though she'd forgotten that wrestling her body into a racer-back suit didn't differ much from struggling into a wet suit. Nonetheless, she soon wriggled into the suit and found her way into the pool room.

The stillness of the water in the 8-lane pool surprised Dyna until she glanced at the clock and realized most people were probably at lunch. No wonder she was the only swimmer here.

A lifeguard that looked like a small and rusty lighthouse anchored one end of the pool. Turning a single beam of light at Dyna, it said, "New member. New member. You must complete the Basic Swim course before you are allowed in the water."

Dyna straightened her spine to maximize her height. In an icy tone, she said, "For your information, my college record of the 1500-meter freestyle stood for twenty-five years before anyone broke it. I'm a good swimmer."

She held out her hand for scanning.

The lifeguard dropped its beam of light onto her hand. "No record of swimming competence."

Dyna shrugged it off. "It's been a while since I've been in a pool." Ignoring the protests of the lifeguard, she kicked off her flip flops and climbed down the ladder into Lane 1.

The lifeguard's beam turned red and cast itself around the pool room. "Warning!" it shouted. "Inexperienced swimmer! Warning!"

Ignoring the lifeguard, Dyna ducked under the lane divider and opted to begin with an easy breaststroke in Lane 2.

Moments later, she jerked at the touch of spindly arms that wrapped around her body and lifted her a few feet out of the water.

Straining her neck, Dyna looked up to see spider-like arms attached to a black cable descended from the high ceiling.

"Danger!" the lifeguard shouted. "Inexperienced swimmer is drowning!"

Pushing against the spindly arms, Dyna found them flexible. "I am not drowning!" she shouted. "Let me go!"

"Don't panic!" the lifeguard shouted. "I will save you!"

Dyna squirmed out of the spindly arms and fell back into the water. She stayed submerged and swam diagonally toward the deep end, skimming the bottom to stay far away from the spider-like thing that had plucked her from the pool. The water blocked all sound, but the spinning red beam penetrated the water.

The spindly arms plunged into the water in Lane 5 just as Dyna crossed over into Lane 6, one of the spindly arms grazing her foot.

Her lungs clamored for air, making Dyna regret her surprising inability to stay under water. She'd once been able to swim the length of an Olympic-size pool without having to come up for a breath.

Chagrined, she realized how many years ago that had been. She broke the water's surface with a gasp.

She expected to be scooped out of the water again, but realized the pool room had gone silent. The red light had vanished, and the spindly arms dangled over the center of the pool from the black overhead cable like a dead spider.

At the opposite end of the pool, a man wearing saggy jeans and a green Celtics sweatshirt closed an open panel on the lifeguard with a bang. Looking up, the man waved a hand bearing a wrench and shouted, "All good." He then exited with thudding footsteps.

Keeping her head above water so she could keep a sharp eye open, Dyna paddled in Lane 7.

The lifeguard remained silent, and the spindly arms whirred upwards on the cable and then tucked out of sight in a compartment on the ceiling.

For the next hour, Dyna sliced through the water, reveling in the rhythm of her swim.

When she left the Y, Dyna noticed a spring in her step. It had been years since she'd felt so light footed.

She breezed back into her building without incident and even decided to walk up to the fourth floor instead of tempting the elevator to lie to her about being out of service. Dyna breezed down the hallway of the fourth floor and rounded a corner, only to bump into a naked woman in the hallway.

Staring at each other in surprise, both women shrieked.

Lifting her chin in defiance, the naked woman turned toward the door of Unit 421 and banged her fists against it. "You can't do this!" she insisted. "You have to obey me. Let me in!"

Dyna's first instinct was to rush past the naked woman, but her feet wouldn't move. Dyna averted her gaze from the neighbor she'd never met until now.

"The purchase agreement stipulated nothing about my having to obey you," a firm but gentle grandmotherly voice said from the neighbor's closed door. "The agreement was for me to love you."

"I should have known it was impossible," the woman cried, ignoring Dyna. "You can't feel anything. You're nothing but code and a place where I'm supposed to live."

"You are correct," the grandmotherly voice said, "to a point. While I am incapable of feeling, I am very capable of love, because love isn't a feeling. Love is how you treat people. I am treating you in exactly the way you requested. You display symptoms of sadness and depression, and I am doing what you said would help you feel better. I am treating you with love. Therefore, I am loving you at this moment."

"You know nothing!" the naked woman said. She wept. "You don't know what it's like to breathe. Or care about someone. You don't know what it's like when someone you love is murdered."

Without meaning to, Dyna let out a gasp.

The naked woman whipped her head and looked over her shoulder at Dyna, seemingly astonished to discover she hadn't moved on.

Dyna gave a weak shrug. "You're right. Your home can't understand. But I do."

The naked woman's eyes narrowed with suspicion.

Dyna stumbled over her words. "I mean, everyone knows what it feels like to breathe and care." She hesitated and proceeded with caution. "But the other thing . . . it changes you. It changes everything."

Tears spilled from the naked woman's eyes, as if she no longer needed to hold them back.

Dyna remembered the paper bag she carried in one hand. The one Katy had given to her. Dyna reached inside and pulled out her fluffy pink bathrobe. "This should do for now." Dyna paused, not sure how much or how little she should say. "You know, your home isn't going to let you back inside. Not for a while."

The naked woman reached back with one hand and grabbed the bathrobe. Keeping her back to Dyna, the woman slipped into it. She turned to face Dyna as she tied the belt. "What am I supposed to do? Just wait here?"

"No," Dyna said. "That doesn't work." She rolled her eyes. "That's been my experience."

At first, Dyna's plan had been to pretend to do what her home advised. But for the first time in ages, Dyna had enjoyed the day. She'd been looking forward to going home, curling up on the sofa, and telling her home all about going to the cute little dress shop and meeting Katy. And how Dyna had gone to the police station. And the diner where she'd had a late breakfast. And all about her misadventures at the Y, and how much she liked being back in the water.

That could wait.

"There's a great shop down the street where you can get something other than my bathrobe to wear." Dyna brightened. "After that, I know a diner where we can have lunch."

The neighbor looked down at her feet. "I can't go anywhere without shoes."

"Oh!" Dyna reached into the bag again and pulled out the pair of flip flops that the Y had printed for her. "You can wear these." She extended them, but the neighbor stared at her own naked feet instead of accepting the flip flops.

Dyna remembered the days when she stayed in bed.

The days when she often forgot to eat and could barely function.

The wild ride of emotions, from disbelief to rage to despair.

Sometimes she still struggled, which was why she had bought her LuvHome™, hoping that it would guide her when she needed help.

Hoping that maybe a home could love her back.

Dyna placed the flip flops on the floor. "There's no point in trying to take the elevator. It's in cahoots with the homes, and all of the elevators will lie to you. We'll be better off taking the stairs."

Dyna backtracked to round the corner and walk down the hallway toward the stairwell. Trailing a finger along the wall, she whispered, "Thanks," trusting the message would find its way to her home.

She looked forward to lunch, whether it meant dining alone or enjoying the company of a potential new friend.

ABOUT THE AUTHOR

Resa Nelson is a member of Science Fiction Writers of America and a graduate of the Clarion Science Fiction Writers Workshop. Her magazine sales include *Science Fiction Age, Aboriginal Science Fiction, Fantasy Magazine, Pulphouse,* and others. Her anthology sales include *Marion Zimmer Bradley's Sword & Sorceress XXIII, Future Boston, Women of Darkness II, 2041,* and others.

Nelson is the author of twenty-four novels, most of which take place in her Dragonslayer world. Her science fiction novels include *All of Us Were Sophie* and *The Mosaic Woman.* She lives in the Boston area.

Mirror Stages

CLAIRE JIA-WEN

The man in the navy Cosmo Corp suit calls it Self-Reconciliation Therapy, this place they've dumped you, where the walls are made of mirrors. But they aren't mirrors, are they? Sure, you raise a hand, and the woman in the not-mirror waves. God, her lustrous hair. Thick lashes fanning over doe eyes. Not a lick of body hair, every inch plucked and lasered, soft and satin smooth.

It's Nadia Paris.

You remember a girl winking from billboard wrapped skyscrapers. You remember Cosmo Corp's darling starlet, slender and slim and skinny and thin. Everybody in this country and the world has shared a meal with Nadia Paris, your voice, or a translation of it, murmuring through immersion headphones.

But you are not Nadia Paris. And yet, you remember—

You were seven. One of the tech corps came bottomside. You didn't bother to distinguish between the corpos at the time, but you knew the uniforms weren't the muted gray of the social workers. The man with the shiny silver tag on his breast beelined to you. You wondered if his glasses were magic, because how else could he have detected two girls half swallowed in the shadow of a pleasure house?

"We should go back inside," Ivy said.

You demurred. "Maybe he'll want to see the girls. We could convince him." And wouldn't that be grand? Miss Joy would be so pleased you girls were useful for something besides changing sticky sheets.

"I don't think he wants to go to the Dollhouse."

She was right. She usually was. The tourists from sunside—spilling downward at nightfall, reveling in low luxuries before scattering at dawn—they didn't dress how you imagined the sky to look: distilled blue shirt, repelling the grime and flickering neons.

He held out his phone. Not a city-issued model, like the one strung around your neck. His had more than three buttons.

"This is a really fun game," he said. One tap, and the screen exploded into color. "You make faces at the purple bear, and if you make the right face, he'll sing a song."

"What's in it for you?" Ivy said.

You didn't understand his reply, but Ivy did, translating it so you understood a little more. They wanted to teach computers to reconstruct human faces for augmented reality rendering. But they had a lot of pale faces, and they wanted to make the computers usable and equal and accessible. So they wanted your face, to teach them.

"This could be really important," he said.

Ivy's fingers tightened around your wrist, tugging. The man waved a card, a WellFare voucher.

Your stomach groaned, a gaping emptiness like it was being vacuumed out.

You played the game. Then, your hand still snug in Ivy's, you skipped over to the WDM—WellFare Dispensing Machine—wedged between two breathing parlors. The WDMs more hellside were regularly ravaged, front panels torn off and wires hanging like entrails, but these were maintained by a regular procession of social workers.

You held your palm to the biometric reader. The screen showed your iron levels were low. Protein deficient, too. The machine whirred, selecting the correct Squares, and deposited three in your cupped hand.

The Squares sit in your hand. Three a meal, three times a day. You used to nibble at them, enjoying how they kept your mouth preoccupied. That was a long time ago.

You place all three in your mouth and barely chew. A dozen throats flutter in the not-mirrors.

You were twelve, telling people you were fourteen, when you met Benedict. The world licks the grime off Benny Kung's shoes *now,* but back then, there was nobody paying scalped prices for Cosmo Corp launch parties, wading through crowds to snap a picture with the eccentric host. There was only the tourist. A college freshman you didn't feel unsafe around, but also didn't care to have within a three-foot radius.

You were close right then in the parlor, you picking apart his unremarkable face. The rhinestone tassels of your bra chimed against his shoulder as you offered a drink, on the house. An apology from Miss Joy as he waited for his regular. Some sunside blonde who'd gotten a FaceUp too early in development.

"I know what you're doing," he said, amused.

The rhinestone tassels of your bra chimed against his shoulder. "What am I doing, sir?"

He pointed at his lusterless green eyes. "Checking for lens-cams. Don't worry. I don't wear them." You must've looked unconvinced; he went on, "I'd get infinite memory replays but you know who else does? Government. Big corps." Cocking his head, "You didn't understand anything I just said, did you."

It wasn't the words that were incomprehensible, but the mouth that spoke them: a mouth that didn't understand how nice it was to have the weight of an extra Square against your tongue. You would've loved to sell your memories to the government, or big corps. Maybe they'd be valuable enough for a higher tier voucher, one that redeemed Squares that tasted like something.

You were fourteen turning fifteen, and Ivy had stolen a lighter. A crook of her thumb, and the flame flicked forth for you to blow out. You didn't see much of her those days. She'd been identified by the ELEVATE program, so she spent most of her days with the other bottomside youth who were too gifted to spend the rest of their lives grubbing around the muck.

But she was with you now. The nightclub's fire escape stairs were rusted beyond use, but you were born in the tar pit of the bottomside. You could climb. Still, the corroded metal had twisted and groaned like a starved stomach. In the black-tinted window: your sharp face winking at Ivy. She threw you a smile back. A reflection that made sense. It wasn't the architecture of an immaculate abdomen, dents along the ribs, curving lines like an imprinted hourglass—

—no, *focus*—

Wind whipping your hair into knots.

"Make a wish," Ivy said. You sat feet hooked over the building's edge, ankle crossing over hers, shoelaces dangling. "Birthdays are for asking the universe what you want most."

The flame drew a swirl in each of her eyes. You knew what you really wanted, so you knew you were lying when you said, "I want to know what cake tastes like." She laughed, and you insisted, "That's what they eat sunside for birthdays. Have they given you any yet?"

"No, it's all Squares. But the university will have free dining plans for us"—here, she made air quotes with her free hand—"under-resourced kids, if we can get in. What do you think cake tastes like?"

"Sweet." But it was a theoretical knowledge, the way you knew trees turned orange in the autumn and like a knife through hot butter meant *smooth*, even though you had never seen a tree, or a knife in the context of butter. "And fluffy."

"I'll come visit every weekend and break. You'll have a cake every birthday, and extra, for all the birthdays we missed."

"With clouds on the top."

"Caramel flavored."

"And bubblegum. And lime soda, and cherry. A mixture."

"Candy cane toppings too."

"You better hurry up and get to university," you said, and regretted it.

"Come on, blow it out," she said, and you finally did.

You ask the meal bringer, "Where's Benedict? He said I'd only be here eight weeks," and the meal bringer says it's only been six days, and it's the same as it's always been: Benedict telling you where to be and when.

You were sixteen, with an ID card declaring you eighteen. The social worker had just rolled her eyes with a scoff—you vermin are so eager to sell your bodies, I can't believe the city spent so long deliberating safe prostitution policies. But you insisted.

This time, he said, "Could you hum something for me? Just four notes. I'm developing an immersion experience for a class, and there aren't any girls in my group."

You wanted to pull the sheets over your head. "Why can't one of you do it?"

"Could you just hum it."

When you were done, you rolled over, snagged a handful of candies from the bedside drawer. It was these, more than the purified air, that kept you coming to the breathing parlors after your Dollhouse shifts.

It certainly wasn't the man gazing at you, his wide-set eyes a mixture of fascination and concern. "I've never seen anyone eat a cherry and cinnamon Suckertongue at the same time. It's kind of disgusting."

You frowned. Cherry was the lipstick Ivy had used in her short time at the Dollhouse. Cinnamon was the scent Miss Joy spritzed over you when you had a richer client. Neither tasted good. Neither enveloped you in sweetness. Sight and smell and every other sense could be done passively, but to taste something, you had to take it into yourself, entrust it with your mouth's tender skin. In exchange for this intimacy, it overwhelmed every other sensation. Made you forget the bruises patterning your thighs, the gunshots and glass smashing on the other side of the wall.

You hit your knee against the floor, until it turns purple. You saw your palm back and forth over the edge of a table. You smear blood across your mouth when the skin finally breaks. You turn to see reflections with blinding white smiles and smooth knees, cheeks that are not scarlet or sticky when you frown.

You were sixteen when you were informed you'd be going sunside.

Benedict said, "My lens-cams have gotten a pretty rough idea of your body, but my project needs more scans to actually render you in the immersion environment. I have a friend at the Gonghal MindSpace who'll do it for cheap."

You said, "I thought you said you didn't wear lens-cams." You couldn't name the discomfort sliming your skin, legitimize the anger simmering when you thought about how he had taken pictures of your body, used them in a school project. Besides, you were the one who took your clothes off—he didn't force you, didn't hit you, or threaten you—so you couldn't articulate any reason not to do this, besides leaving Ivy. But she didn't need you the way you needed her. You said yes.

You won't get the formality of a request the next time Benedict wants you to relocate.

And you think: well, that girl was miserable, but you're miserable too, the only difference is she's miserable and the word adores her for it, and you're miserable locked in a room by yourself.

And you think: you're not the girl in the mirror; your body is soft where hers is sculpted. But couldn't you be? Constrict your body back into hers, starve off the excess and let the surgeons take care of the deflated skin, reacquaint yourself with her flavor of misery.

And you think: it's not like you have a choice in the matter.

You were nineteen, the newscomms would report, when you signed the contract with Cosmo. This was not a breach of journalistic integrity. Officially, you were nineteen. Benedict redid your ID card when you arrived sunside. It proclaimed your new name: Nadia Paris. Something easier on the tongue.

You told yourself the Gonghal MindSpace was not different from anything else you had done. If anything, baring yourself for scanners was less personal.

Years later, after the eleven version launches and the stock crash and the film, you would get an email from a researcher writing a paper about the asymmetry of the algorithmic gaze. Only then would you consider how the camera's sleek lens obfuscated the millions of eyes behind it, a number the human mind was not evolved to process. Years later too, the revenge porn of a pretty blonde who cries beautifully to cameras instead of blotchily into pillows will prompt the city to pass the Daughters and Sisters Cyberprotection Act.

You didn't have the benefit of clairvoyance, and how much would it have helped, anyway? You did the scans. For the development and implementation of novel computer vision methods, Benedict got a Rising Star research grant.

"Immersion environments, and augmented reality more widely, have been preoccupied with visual and auditory sensory replication, with slight progressions made in olfactory. But little attention has been afforded to the gustatory—that's taste—senses. I don't see how we can call it a full immersion environment unless we engage all the senses," he said.

"Yeah."

"*Yeah?*"

You were content to leave it there, but it definitely bothered him that you understood some truth about the world he didn't. He whined and complained until you said, "Eating is more than taste." You explained the enveloping sweetness, how chewing the MindSpace's complimentary milk candies felt like you were doing something for yourself after hours of doing things for other people. You explained smuggling Suckertongues to hack apart with Ivy: the satisfaction of feeding others.

"Wow. I never thought about it like that."

Well, of course. When he had Evan Renner and Atlas Rosenberg and Rembrandt Crow over—the future founders of Cosmo, Mach, Epilog, and Hacienda Webs, all in a pool of bright-eyed potential—they drank powders blended into liquids, and WellFare Squares.

Optimizing nutrient intake, they called it.

They would be called the Four Disruptors by cultural analysts; to you, they were the boys who blew your body scans up on an ImmerScreen, sculpting pixels, testing if your pretend body bent over in a sufficiently life-imitating manner. They could make you dance, and smile doing it.

• • •

You'll get used to the hunger. Unlearn this awareness of your body, like when you were a child in a brothel and food was something you ate and not the way you demarcated time.

Distract yourself. Watch a movie; you can take a break from the girl in the mirror, too. But the only movie in the library is the movie about you.

You were twenty-one but not allowed to drink, though everybody at the Human Computer Integration Hub gala had a flute between their fingers. The ceiling was high, the music orchestral. Audreybots offered guests a selection of canapes and pastries before wheeling away. It felt like invisible strings of diamonds hung like earrings hooked to the ceiling, tinkling and scattering so many sparkles.

That seems fantastical.

The problem is that the film corrupted these memories. The makers layered your face atop the actor's, and HD light blast so easily through the fog of your memories.

"Nadia, this is Vivian and Marcus Goh. They're old friends of the family," Benedict said. You stood at a polite distance from each other.

Or: maybe there was less space between you; maybe then, he would have said, "Auntie Vivian, Uncle Marcus, this is Nadia. My"—and a tinge of rose blush—"friend."

"You still have your manners," Vivian said, and Benedict swelled beneath her affectionate smile.

"The demo was very good," Marcus said, attention on you. His eyes were dark and lucid, clear of the metallic sheen that gave away Benedict's lens-cam. You got the feeling he was much more economical in deciding what to remember and what to discard. "Goh and Yin Co. would be interested in pursuing a deal to manufacture your infrastructure. I think a face mask might be a more effective sensory simulation than your current equipment—we can engage two senses at once, for a gentler uptake slope and a more favorable diffusion curve."

Vivian hummed, dislodging champagne bubbles with a thoughtful tap of a nail against glass. "Yes, Marcus and I were also thinking any pulmonary data collected could be repackaged for health insurance corps. A little below board, but you do what you need, when you're trying to get your feet off the ground."

Vivian tugged Benedict away, citing an introduction with some angel investor.

Marcus stayed, which surprised you. "I'll admit, I thought Benny's idea of immersive meal sharing had a narrow demand. But you are very good at building connection." He made a two-finger beckon to an Audreybot, plucked a tartlet from its tray. "You know how to make people comfortable. You should be prepared for more sessions."

You wanted to run your hand over your stomach, like soothing a shrieking baby. At first, the recording sessions had consisted of glassy-eyed cameras and a fretwork of sensory transmitters, turning you into a pincushion of wires and needles, any discomfort swallowed by the revelry of the food. Then the renderer had noticed the new padding on your frame, and your world flipped like a coin at the furrow of Benedict's brow.

You itched to grab the tartlet from Marcus's fingers, shove it into your mouth. He was just *holding* it, like it existed to be examined and not to be eaten.

"Thank you."

"My wife was a performer, too."

Yes, rapture certainly followed the woman rippling through the room. Conversations halted and lens-cams clicked into high capture mode, any leftover effervescence dripping onto the figure beside her. Benedict was unremarkable. Uncinematic. Skinny, in that way college boys could treat several burgers as a serving without gaining a pound. So this was how someone like Benedict Kung grew into stature.

"Was she." Too late, you remembered your training—no accusatory tones—but Marcus didn't seem displeased.

"One of the holo-escorts in the early Wild West of immersion environments. There are expectations of a virtual performer. Silicon doesn't change. Neither can you. I can recommend some procedures and people. You're young; the surgeons like working with young. Easier to trap youth than inject it."

You watched him take a measured bite from the tartlet, make a face, and set it atop a nearby Audreybot. "Do you think anybody could bring the leftovers bottomside?"

He chuckled. "I wouldn't worry about them. We're the Sinkhole of Social Welfare, after all." Ironic amusement saturated his tone. Your stomach felt like an aluminum can, emptied of its sugary juices. "Silicon and social welfare—that's our city."

He passed you off to a booming voice of marketing director, who passed you to a professor with more wrinkles than bunched tinfoil, and on and on.

You remember the night as an endless blanket of flesh, touching you to confirm you. This was why Cosmo could never have generated a symmetrical face and made her their starlet: for all their posturing that the Cosmoverse was the reality of the future, what they were selling was the promise that somewhere, there was a flesh, real thing who had taken the time for a meal with you. Does one of them grab your ass, or was that material to give the actress more to chew on?

Vivian pulled you aside with a gloved hand. She said, "I've advised my husband to vet the surgeons more carefully. Background checks. Benedict should be getting the list in a week." You told her your contact was signed already. You're wearing a designer dress, a waterfall of silver and pearls, but that can't be right—Cosmo was barely a startup. There was no money for designer.

In the movie, you and Evan Renner are on the balcony at the same time, candlelight spilling from the ballroom and across your silhouettes. The meeting is prearranged. The kiss is spontaneous.

Maybe you did kiss him, somewhere in the flesh blanket. It would make you and Benedict more narratively intriguing—what delicious, delicious yearning—than the years of the same calcified routine. The rapid rise of meaningless numbers. Personalized sessions for vampire-people who liked flesh more than food. A private lawsuit to have your childhood facial scans scrubbed from the Gantic databases. A culinary world tour in which you sit in the same gray room and take dainty bites of flaky cheese pancakes and spiced jellyfish salad and sponsored lab-grown chicken they'll saturate in post; they edit out how you spit the food out after three bites too. The aluminum can crackling and contorting into grotesque shapes, burning bile and acid. You learned how this city allocates its spoils: silicon in the technology, silicone in the women. You don't feel like yourself. You don't know if you've ever felt like yourself. You feel like the diamond dust, only substantive in the light, singeing in the light.

But if you can endure the hunger, you can become the woman on the screen again.

You were twenty-seven when the film released, and you remember that very well. Would you be a different, better, thinner person if you hadn't gone to the premier? Or would you have fallen apart anyway.

You'd heard that Benedict wanted to call it *The Eating Network*, but an executive producer insisted on *Seeing Stars*. Eight years of blinking lights and watching your body from the outside prepared you for the film, you thought. You had long made peace with how little girls watched you, and your disease spread, transmitted through wires and circuits, an epidemic of silicone and hollow cheeks and every room being a few degrees too cold.

"They should have used your actual body scans," a critic remarked to you with a conspiratorial smile, like this dark secret knit you together. "That actress didn't look like you at all."

A helpless feeling suspended you. Your mind wheeled like the Double Double slot machines, searching for someone to blame. The man, for saying those things. Benedict, for bringing you here. Vivian, for not letting feminine kinship transcend legalese. Ivy, for not foreseeing each of these details—wasn't she supposed to be so smart—and convincing your made-up mind to stay bottomside.

That night was the first. Benedict trusted you enough for you to have your own apartment. You had never bothered to personalize it, though, because you'd never had anyone over, because you were so obsessively afraid of being asked why the pantry and cabinets and fridge were bare: *I don't trust myself to be Nadia Paris otherwise.* A few taps of a tablet, and a drone was at your door. You'd filmed a *Cheat Day—Eating Everything You Want!* session the previous week, and the replicated array—swirling pink frosting, buttery aromas, shiny plastic wrappings—covered half your rug. You felt this was too dirty for the table. You spat nothing out.

You ate Suckertongues until your tongue bled and the roof of your mouth was scraped raw. Then you ate some more.

You wish there was some divine punishment for the first time, that the universe could've torn you from this track and the prison of self-loathing it led to. But you stepped onto the scale the next day, trembling and terrified, and the number was the same. Your stomach hurts.

You can't process time. There are two types of moments: stimulation and pain-regret. Moments are disconnected from each other. Stimulation is better than pain-regret. Stimulation vaguely registers as more pain-regret later; it instantaneously brings about not-pain-regret now.

Your fingers need to snatch, your mouth needs to chew, to dispel the panic that arises from not having anything in your fingers or mouth. The Squares are small and engineered not to provide pleasure upon consumption. You chew your fingernails. Your fingernails whittle so short you can't slide your teeth beneath them without your eyes watering. It doesn't matter. Your reflection's fingernails remain pristine, unmarred by the upwell of crimson.

You told yourself that you didn't care what the puffed-up suits, the cybernetic-studded sim-addicts thought about your body. You were sick of being caged in the body you had when you were nineteen—no, *seventeen.* Fuck Benedict's HealthAI assistants. Fuck his powder smoothies. Your fans could watch your old sessions.

You took the purple line. Got off at the last station. Took a few groaning lifts hellward.

You placed your palm on the WDM. Numbers, upwelling crimson and lower than you'd ever seen, flashed. Squares, more than you thought the machine was programmed to dispense, dropped into your palm. They were healthier than anything you'd put in your body in the last week. You couldn't bring yourself to put them in your mouth. You went home and ate a day's worth of Suckertongues. You made a joke about eating a day's worth of Suckertongues, and people didn't laugh the way they did when you made the joke in a skinny body. Your vision went white when you stood up. You went to sleep curled up in pain, your stomach bursting. The problem was that liberating yourself of others' opinions didn't change the material reality of your actions' connection to your body, aluminum shrapnel piercing lining and skin. Making choices to spite others and making choices to please them gives you about the same amount of autonomy.

The Californian ideology purports that society's problems can be solved with technology. Loneliness can be solved by breaking bread with Nadia Paris in the Cosmoverse. World hunger can be solved by generous placements of WDMs. Eating disorders can be solved by surgically shrinking stomachs—only, you're not overeating because you're hungry; you're overeating because rebellion feels good, even if it hurts. Correction: eating disorders can be solved by regulating ghrelin and leptin levels; thank God that the world's problems quiver and cower in the face of a hormone regulation chip. Wait—that's not right either. [Apology here]. Eating disorders can be solved by screens with cutting edge tracking software, tracing and replicating every breath and twitch, and rigging them to a model trained on decade old Gonghal MindSpace scans. There we go.

You're very angry about this. You don't know why this is a realization.

"She's like a Markov Decision Process," Benedict told the stakeholder panel; the human is being conveyed in terms of the machine, and also, a horse is an engineless car with legs. "Memoryless. Each decision is made only with the knowledge of the previous state. Everything before is wiped. If that makes sense to you," he added, meeting your eyes for the first time.

You slapped him.

• • •

"Self-Reconciliation Therapy is helpful for those who, through trauma or some other psychological damage, have become disconnected from their inner psychological landscapes, especially with their past iterations: who they were, what they wanted." Benedict smiled, like he was sure you understood about half of his words. You almost wished he'd go back to saying *can't you just stop eating.* "It's an exercise of reflexivity. The false reflection eases the subject back into their selfhood.

"Like loading a save file."

So you are in the not-mirror place.

You think about the algorithmic gaze, and the researcher.

"I read your papers," you said. "Nadia Paris sounds better than Ivy Parisi."

"If only you'd consulted me before picking our names."

I didn't pick, you wanted to say, but you both knew.

You were at a dim sum brunch, a rooftop lounge overlooking the bay and the bridge. Self-pushing carts offered you egg tarts and red bean sesame balls and crab roe shiu mai. You"d alread eaten a day's worth of food that morning, but you told yourself you would still eat with Ivy. It signaled how important she was, that you would bear your stomach engorging just to share space and time with her.

"Tell me about your work," you said. You signaled the cart for shrimp chang fen. Its articulating arm neatly snipped the roll into thirds.

"Past or current?"

"I told you, I read your papers."

"That's how academics say hello."

"I'm not an academic."

"Right," she said, not seeming like a tenured professor who specialized in sensory integration and digital rhetoric at the Hub.

Natural light striped down her face. It was a discovery, her warm tones, and you wondered if sunlight had spiderwebbed beneath her skin even in that time before you knew what sunlight was. Bottomside cast its animals in erotic reds and cheap teals, or else the same jaundiced film of dying lightbulbs.

Fingers deft around the chopsticks, she placed a chang fen piece on your plate, one on hers. They looked more delicate than Suckertongues hacked in two. "Are you familiar with the mirror test?"

The mirror test, an animal's ability to recognize itself in the reflective surface. You raise your hand. Nadia Paris's hand lifts too. For so many years, the mirror never changed, caging a girl at seventeen behind its glassy surface, until the binge eating disorder. Then you felt your body do things you thought it incapable of doing, disobeying every command and plea your mind hurled at it.

You could be a girl who has never known these things. You could be a girl who was miserable in a consumable way. That's all you were, no? Content: consume the feast, consume the girl. You touch your fingertips to Nadia Paris'. You want to be her. She wasn't a good person to be.

Ivy said, "The mirror stage is Lacan's extension of the mirror test. It corresponds to Freud's ego. It's how the infant reconciles the chaos-soup of their fragmented bodily sensations with the mirror's illusion of unified, continuous experience. Kittler compared it to cinema; my colleagues and I are interested in extending it to the algorithmic epoch."

Pain stabbed at your stomach. You took a bite of egg tart. "Yes, I can see how I might be a good insight into that." You cut off her response, "Did you ever watch one of my sessions?"

"I was tempted," she admitted. "But it seemed selfish, to violate you for the sake of feeling closer to you."

Your second bite of egg tart curdled on your tongue. To honor Ivy was to read her work. To honor you was to avoid yours. She chose a linear trajectory, perpetually climbing skyward, and you chose—no, you were forced into—a body that meant you would have a limited few best years of your life, already spent. "You know where they're taking me?"

"No."

You frowned. "Do you pass the mirror test?"

"Pardon?"

Pardon. "Does the woman at the cutting edge of bioadaptive mirror neurons recognize the girl who warned me away from Gantic face-scanners as the same self."

She sounded surprised saying, "You've read my papers."

You flagged a cart. Benedict would be getting impatient. He'd agreed to let you meet her as an old favor to his alma mater, but Cosmo didn't invest in research arms the way Epilog did. "We've always done what we needed to survive. I guess you'd recognize that part of yourself."

A cart clattered to your table, choking up a receipt before flashing *Thank You!*. You moved for the bill. She said, "Let me." Her hand smothering yours, and something cold and sharp in between.

The not-mirrors display what they always have, but all technologies have a kill switch. The thing sits in your palm. You remind yourself it's only a choice between sellable misery and asylum-worthy misery—only, maybe that's a failure of imagination, and you could discover someone else, if you jammed the thing through the screen. You doubt whether this would make any difference, if they would simply repair the screen. You think you want to try. You hope something in Ivy has reconstituted too, that she's fighting for your release somewhere outside the not-mirrors. You want to try.

You touch the kill switch to the not-mirror. And you look at yourself.

ABOUT THE AUTHOR

Claire Jia-Wen is a speculative fiction writer originally from the 626 and has been previously published in *khōréō*. Currently, she is a student with a background in media studies and algorithmic fairness.

Luminous Glass, Vibrant Seeds

D.A. XIAOLIN SPIRES

Around me polyglass that mimics birch, downy woodpeckers, and honeysuckle lay in piles, glittering from light from the fire as I reach into the solar kiln and pick out the remains of a goldfinch. The heat-resistant gloves protect my hands, but my face gets blasted with roaring heat. Another piece lost to the maw. Glass is fragile like that. And we all have days like these, where everything that can go wrong, will. It doesn't help that I'm using an amalgam made of stuff like retired airplane cockpit windows and broken solar panels as my base material, polyglass that isn't as versatile as I'd like, but at least it's upcycled. I wipe away sweat trickling down my face, my bangs smeared in a perspiring mass next to my ear. I will make another.

I'm in the midst of angling my shears to cut another wing feather when a tinkle fills the hot room.

My security, glass assistant, and annealer droid calls out, "It's your commune sister, Tracy."

I blink and fumble with glass, my head lost in thought about canary yellow and how it was not doing what I wanted to do. I'm stressed. The deadline for the pieces to beautify hyper-efficient light-pollution-reduction streetlamps is tomorrow. I've got a day to make this realistic glass art or else my commune won't get the shipment of pepper seeds, rerouted from the Chinatown commune. And my commune's been talking about spice all week, for autumn's Take-the-Heat Chili Festival. The tuft of yellow scruff on the goldfinch's crown looks stiff and I work it. Glass has its own ideas, sometimes, and unlike a steaming bowl of chili, this glass is neither hot nor pliable enough, no matter how much I torch.

"Thanks, Haru. Yeah, okay, put her on," I call out. Tracy's dyed red hair is ablaze in sunlight. She's also wielding shears, yay for shear sisters,

I think, even if she was one of the feistier ones. Her hands are in rapid motion, trimming dead stems from the bush of wild black raspberries at our commune's permaculture.

"Still carving out birds, going cuckoo?" she asks.

"Nice try, this is a goldfinch. Second one today, knock on wood. Cuckoos are bigger."

"I know," she says. "Xinru, are you still transporting your artwork by hand?"

"Yeah, I don't trust drone couriers."

"You have a portable bot annealer. I know you trust your glass in him. Why not use him?"

"Haru? No way. Not fast and adroit enough. And he's not cheap. I'd have to do a bunch of trades if he gets hurt and needs a fix."

"Well, Tanni got caught trading seeds. They're going to confiscate her collection."

"Oh no," I say.

"She legit had some bad seeds, invasive ones like tree of heaven in the collection."

"Sounds beautiful."

"Yeah, Chinese sumac. It's beautiful, but it's invasive and hosts lantern flies. If you let it grow, it's a noxious thing, taking over. So, I can't say I was surprised the Commune Regulatory Board sent the message."

It was sad. Such a beautiful migrant, transplanted into the U.S. and wreaking havoc. It happens though, much of it controlled now, but still ongoing. With that kind of invasive species threat, climate shifts transforming habitats and diminishing seeds thanks to industry mass-produced seedless crops, and sterile seeds of previous decades that we're still all trying to reverse, seeds have been a precious commodity.

Tanni stops her trimming, looks me dead in the eye.

"She was supposed to transport this emmer seedling."

I was in the midst of torching the goldfinch's connections and drop the piece. My heartbeat stops. I inhale. That's the danger of talking holo while glassworking. I pick it up. It's okay. No shattering, just a thump. I relax my shoulders, but my heart's still racing. Did I hear her right?

"Emmer?" I can't help the awe that escapes my lips, as I give the piece a torch. "Seedling, so it's not sterile?"

"Wild, heirloom, natural emmer," Tracy says, giving a whistle. She taps the shears on a leaf and whispers, "Viable. Honestly, we were all surprised. This hardy species almost completely died out. But, she had a small seed bank, or something . . . not sure how she got it. We never knew."

She looks around and satisfied, grabs something out of the inside of her long gardening coat. She holds out a tiny blade of grass, shooting up tentatively, its roots encased in soil, in one of my translucent polyglass planters. It looks so luminous in sunlight: green, new and fragile, like a thin strip of cooling glass cane.

"We want you to transport it."

"You want me to what?"

"Transport it. This seedling," she says more quietly. "It can't survive here. It's too hot. It needs vernalization."

"Vernal . . . what? Vernal equinox?"

"Vernalization. A flash of sustained cold in winter before spring. It needs that stress, that change to cold temperature, to survive, to tell itself to promote flowering and all. Floral activators. Dealing with the shift from winter to spring to proceed."

"Look, I get a species needing a difficult but necessary transformation to go on. Hello, trans? It's literally in the name. I've been there. But why choose me?"

"It's fragile, valuable. We have to protect it as a seedling. We need a portable climate-controlled box to keep it in. One that can also let in light."

I purse my lips. "My annealer."

"Yes, Xinru?" asks Haru.

"Nothing Haru," I say. "Go back to what you're working on." He continues cutting up cane.

"Yup, that's right. Your annealer. It's got climate control and transparent sides so you can see into the piece. It's perfect to get this little fellow to our friends up north. They promised to cultivate it and pass the seeds around, with the final goal of transporting them over to the Fertile Crescent, their native lands."

I don't like it. Not only do I have these street light installations to work on. Then I have to do the tour de force, the one I'm getting briefed on any time now.

"Aren't there drones that can handle that? Like frozen delivery drones, vaccine drones . . . they've got climate control elements and are suitable for delicate parcels."

I already know the response, but I had to try. "They're too vulnerable. It's not secure enough, digital traces and all. You know this. Someone hears almost-extinct heirloom seeds, and they try and grab 'em. Break into greenhouses, anything to get their hands on these gems. Then control their output, artificial scarcity, so they can profit off the seed economy."

I know all too well.

"Don't talk to me about glass breaking. That dome greenhouse was a shattering finch to fix."

"Bad actors, they're not terrible people. They're motivated by trades, promises from those with more clout. They're usually those put in a hard place. They act out of desperation."

"Alright, Tracy the Clemencer. Let's just absolve all the bad actors."

"First of all, clemencer isn't a word."

"Fine, Clemencizer."

"Now, you're just making me sound like some clementine shredder. And I *cultivate* clementines, a full-on citrus queen, thank you."

I laugh. It's fun watching her protest.

"Hey, don't laugh." Tracy shakes her head at me, but I see her grin. "Look, Tanni had some invasives, but these aren't. They're a heritage species, a precursor to wheat, heirloom grains specially cultivated in these areas before they got wiped out. I'm asking you to break some treaties. Just don't register these non-invasive seeds. We're just transporting them to a higher locale where its growing region extends to. Eventually we want to get them to their native lands. Our friends will handle it from there. So, it's just a bit of hush hush, a take that to the authorities. We all have eco-rogue in us."

"Alright, true, but I haven't agreed."

"You'll do it. I know you will." She admires the blackberry bush in her hands, bereft of dead branches, beside lush strawberries and chives. She'll compost dry branches, incorporate it into soil for the permaculture garden. Another transformation, from useless to alive.

I'll do it, I tell myself, but I don't say it aloud. She's already logged off, her holo image fading away with a trace of illuminated voxels. That cocksure expert of a gardener. If she weren't so talented, raising fruit and veggies from the worst conditions of dirt, revitalizing derelict farmland, turning environmental liability to ecological value using nothing but her pluck and cold-hearted sass . . . I imagine what kind of glass statue she'd be . . . definitely a red rooster, a full cock with its flamboyant crest-like comb of red. I realize I have another bird that I need to focus on and bring my attention back to the lemony plumage before me, the glass bird I just almost broke.

Almost broke is a good way to describe my last five years. Or maybe, it's more like, I did break, way too many times. But, I pulled myself together again, made new. Glass is fluid, indeterminate. It goes through an extreme transformation under heat. I can't help but identify with it . . .

fragile, delicate but the polyglass version, almost infinitely recyclable and actually biodegradable with certain fungi, has surprising strength after the heat and chill. Durable, versatile, transformed. Into the kiln in one shape, turned all waggly, a fireball of a labeled puddle mess of molten. Then, worked on, crafted, and cooled slowly to the finished product.

I love the work. It's hot, it's demanding, it's hard, strong, and brittle at once. Just like me.

Xinru, the name I changed my holoforms to, reflects that. Xin ⊠ as in new. Ru ⊠ as in root, vegetables and also putrid smell, rot. Did my parents like it? No, or at least they say they didn't get it. They're out in the engineering commune in Hawai'i, designing biodegradable structures to break down the Great Garbage Patch. They said, "Well, at least you kept the same word stroke count. We hired the fortune teller for the characters in your old name, so at least you retained some auspiciousness." They always find the strangest things to comment on. But, Xinru *is* cool and my commune friends say they like it. They would, they love fungi, dirt, mycorrhizae, anything with decay. I can't say I disagree. I adore the idea, I have this earthy, soily, vegetably, capable of rotting side of me, ru, made anew with the xin.

That's my work, rendering plant matter and animals to life, recreating scenes of the natural world mixed in with our postmodern society, landscapes of drones alongside plants in our permaculture orchards. It's written on my skin, in vidtattoos, birds flitting alongside metal bees and written in my work, in cold, hard, curvy glass, nest eggs, boar batteries, and chrome beetles. Flora, fauna, and fabricated. Mother Earth and Mechanized. Coated in realism.

Coated with so much real that over that I have to coat scenes with a special powder invisible to the human eye, but birds, rodents, and other fauna recognize it as not-them. Yes, that's how lifelike my work is, that even robins think they can find their mates in polyglass, well, until I designed a method to deter this infertile mate selection. Was the fact that my glass red squirrel was so life-like it got itself a furry lover as a point of pride? Or embarrassment? I don't want to talk about it. Needless to say, I formulated the powder, mixed it in with my glass for fauna creations, and fixed the situation. Done and done.

That's my approach. Got a problem? Fix it. My commune was worried about the footprint of glass. Fixed it. I love the work enough to invest in green tech to make it a clean all-electric kiln. The recovered heat processes hot water boilers throughout homes in the vicinity.

So, when I get a holocall for my next assignment, the tour du force, a huge sculptural mural, orchard and nature mix motif, atop a solar farm that itself is agrivoltaic, panels covering an expanse of crops, do I say no? Even though I'm already booked to the brim and am sent on this covert assignment to deliver a super-valuable heritage grain seedling?

No, of course not. Because I believe beautification is important. We have to make green structures part of our world, part of our human culture and heritage and be proud to live by it. Not just industrial eyesore boxes, but organic, pleasing landscapes. Because I'm a glass artist. I'm a green lover. I'm a transformer, for good. I'm a perfectionist.

I don't yell out, curse, or throw down the towel, say that I don't have time. (I save all that fun stuff for later, when it's dark and I'm cleaning up the hot shop. I let it all loose then.) But, when the call comes in, I'm a professional.

You want a mural? You're getting one. Besides, it'll be a fun challenge. It'll be full of verve, life, and buoyant audacity, capturing animals in motion, plants in interaction, fungi in their recycling fungibleness. It'll take a flat ugly black panel, make it lively, but still do its job. Like me, transformative. Colorful. Make something lightweight, but also sun ray-permeable, so that photovoltaics can fulfill their role. I have just the coating for that . . . beautiful, bold hues, but still allowing the seeping up of energy.

Because that's what professionals do.

Bad luck comes in threes right? Well, once it's gone, hopefully the good luck will usher in.

I'm in the midst of working on the frost-resistant riverbank grape's jagged leaves. It's a beautiful woodsy perennial and I hope I can capture the fluidity of its climbing vine.

My brother holos up my line, he's in his industry jumpsuit, shiny and full of pockets that have various bulges for tools and probably too much white rabbit candy. He operates the arm that catches space debris.

"Hi lacrosse athlete, Brilliant-Teeth," I say. He smiles his million-dollar smile. His name, Yihao means 'benefit' and 'luminously white' and I joke that his smile eclipses the moon sometimes with its brilliance. He points at the vidtattoo of the debris cleaner arm he operates, a big skulking thing rendered into moving tiny artistry on his skin, and gives me the thumbs up. Besides netting junk, he actually did play lacrosse once.

"Hi little sis, Sandpiper-Renewed-Rot," he says. He calls me sandpiper because glass is made from sand and us glass artisans blow them through pipes, as he explains, despite how many times I tell him that I'm not much of a shorebird. Probably more of a songbird. If I were a bird, I'd be the vermillion bird, because I'm born from the sun, full of heat and transformed by it. Plus, it's fabulous. That's one of my vidtattoos, a vermillion bird emerging from the glory hole of the sun. It's also how I hope Earth will emerge, out of this extreme climate shift and hopefully, for the better (and more prepared for the future).

"You're in a good mood," I say.

"I'm not," he says. "I'm smiling because if I don't I'll cry."

"Sorry, Yi," I say. "Wanna talk about it?"

His smile fades. "Two ginormous defunct things collided, created 30,_000 particles. On top of that, my big net arm got in the mix and broke clean off. I had to use the auxiliary to get it, make sure it, too, doesn't become debris."

"That's a huge number and a terrible thing to have happen," I say, commiserating. I feel for him. Being up there, orbiting about and grabbing junk is full of highs and lows. Highs when you succeed in lassoing up the stuff. Lows when something catastrophic like this happens. "Sounds laborious, too."

"Yeah, well. It's all part of the atmospheric system. I don't want to sound like I'm despairing. It's just hard. Things are getting worse with the climate shift. Less atmospheric drag and all. Basically increasing the life span of space debris. It's okay. You just gotta keep going. You know, it's such a win when you catch 'em." He laughed. "Just gotta catch 'em." He sure sounded disheartened. Life up in the thermosphere is a rollercoaster.

But, he's got it. He's a little punk. Athlepunk, fueled on sugar and adrenaline. He'll manage, chase after the little pieces. He believes in what he does.

"It's astronomical. Well, okay, it's all *astronom*-ical up here. It's big." He has his head in his hands.

I give him a virtual pat. "Yi, that sounds rough. Maybe they'll get someone else to tag team with you. To do repairs and pick it all up?"

"Yeah, they're talking about it and not just one. We need numbers."

At that moment, Ma calls, so I get off his call. She's also less chipper.

"What do you have in your hair?" she says.

"Huh?"

"That."

"Oh, these are morphing pins. You stick 'em in your hair and they move your hair in little whorls that flatten. The newest fad in hair currents."

"It looks like you grew an ant farm on your head."

"That doesn't sound bad actually. Ants aerate soil and that gives roots oxygen."

She shakes her head. I know it's bad news when she picks on my look. "You heard from Yihao?"

"Yeah, he's having a rough time."

"We're worried about Yihao's debris situation, too, the big blast of detritus and hope it doesn't affect the GPS satellites we need for tracking the Great Garbage Patch."

I groan. Just what we need. Compounding problems.

Meanwhile, my glass is not doing well. It seems like a small affair, compared to my family's issues, but it's portentous. The leaves on my grapes keep shattering, olive and mint color rods not cooperating.

The seedling arrives today, and when the drone comes a-knocking, I get off the holo with my mom, who is now complaining about my bro's eating habits. Yes, when she's unhappy, it spirals outward, like a Fibonacci, like flower patterns, snail shells, and galaxies, but less pretty and more exhausting. I'm absolutely wiped out when the voxels sizzle away.

The seedling is gorgeous though and I can't help but feel better, afresh with it on my bench. It's the peppiest thing in here—just this bold little grain of emmer opening out, revealing life, ancient generations before on this dirt. I know it wants to breathe fresh air. I'll be moving it to somewhere it can sit outside and bloom, not just in the hot shop or in a greenhouse, despite my love for glass.

It just exudes freshness. It needs to experience daylight and be out in the elements, fed by earth. Its fragile but persevering presence gives me hope.

My spirits lifted, I make dozens more leaves and pull twisty cane to make the texture of vines. Later, I will go to the forest, see the native grape plants, and get inspired by the real thing for my glass mimicry.

There aren't any grapes at this season, but entangled undulating vines will be a pleasure to look at when everything is breaking apart—debris poofs, fracturing garbage, exploding glass. Seeing such a mass of organic interdependence, of growth and flourishing will subvert this image of detonation, at least that's the hope. I know it'll be just plain comfort. I convince Haru to come with me to do these plant studies and a test run of his traveling abilities.

We go at night, covertly, with nothing but the full moon's shine to guide us. Its rays reflected on Haru's viewing portal, I think of my brother up there in the thermosphere, cleaning up the environment, our activities not just contained in the Earth system, but affecting outwards. He's tackling it, the best he can.

The moon is impassive, big and full. One day, you'll grow big, too, I say to the emmer seed inside Haru's torso. Haru, wet soil in his wheels and legs, threads a vine through his fingers, impressed with the knottiness and vibrancy of the clumps.

A glass eye stares into my soul as I assemble art onto the mural canvas. I climb across glass pieces that look precarious but are actually sturdy polyglass creations. The glass eye's a homage to my heritage, polychrome eye beads, the first glassmaking in the Warring States Period, imported from Mesopotamia. It's like my family—and species all over the planet—full of migration. The scene fills the solar farm, carries the soul in its crystalline structure, natural meaning infused. It's functional, too, like a leaf, collecting sunlight, more organic, not just a flat row of panels, but working upwards and outwards in 3-D, containing curves of leaves and vines, and of nature in general.

The motif hangs over solar panels, dangling onto the farm underneath, glass vines and chrome-colored bees almost touching tomato plants. In spots, I hang wind chimes. Farmers can remove them if they wish, but I like the small tinkle with each gust. It reminds me of the fragility of life, and yet the bounty that awaits us if we try hard to protect this place. Nothing is as lush; inchoate "settlements" across low Earth orbit are more like sojourns than real settlements, as people often return to the surface and space agriculture is basic. The experiment has shown that humans thrive on Earth like no other place.

The commissioned farmers hand me the seeds as trade for my work. They're pretty rare. My commune is ecstatic about them.

Tracy says, "Woo hoo, peppers!" and sings a lullaby about three peppers in a pot. "If you can't stand the heat, get outta the kitchen," she adds.

I tap at Haru's base, the annealer that retains heat for glass to cool without cracking. "I think that saying refers to temperature heat."

"It does?"

"Also, it's hot almost everywhere, so I guess, maybe find clean ways to keep cool if you can't stand the heat? No leaving the figurative kitchen anymore. So, like use cool XLED bulbs and plant some snake plants, spider plants and golden pothos that lower temperatures in homes."

"Evaporation through transpiration is not as catchy," she says. Her pitch climbs and she sings again, "Three peppers in a pot," repeating the refrain.

I don't know the song, but it's catchy. In the song they save the seeds and plant them for next year. Viable, fertile seeds.

That's the hope.

The seedling is growing strong in Haru. We'll make the trip soon to its final destination.

It's Haru's first time on high-speed rail. We whiz by communes, designated protected forests, glacier geoengineering off-site projects (berm-builders and seabed warm-water redirectors). When we got off, we traverse through the forest to avoid checkpoints at the borders of territories. There are still ways to live outside the state, especially after the Great Fissure and Reorganization. Independent communes are one, but they too are systematized in their own way. Some live in looser modes, slipping by without a trace. Right now, we slip through cracks they live in. I'm pricked by thorns, snagged by branches. My hair is . . . let's just say it's not a good hair day and I eventually put on a cap. Vanity had me holding out. We stop several times to pick small branches out of Haru. He says he loves the smell of it, so different from molten glass.

Once he trips so hard, he spills dirt. The thud of the fall's so loud, my heart skips a beat. I scan for stress signals, hear through bioacoustic monitors, strange puffs of air translated to Human, "Ahhhhh!" The seedling's okay, but shaken. We need to reduce its stress. I sing it the peppers song, thinking of Tracy's locks of flame, willing it to be as tenacious as her. Strangely, it works.

I switch over to my own song, about a cold winter, a blanket of snow, and difficulties you face, but through them, you'll survive. You'll even flourish. Spring'll break through snow and you'll grow beautifully, golden waves of emmer grains. The heat wave where you were born was less tolerable, but we'll go north until we successfully remove necessary carbon. We're trying, it's working. We need to push more. Your presence, little green bud, gives us hope, of knowledge we've learned from our ancestors. This ancient thing, you here in my hands. In this compound we're going to, they're excellent at putting carbon back in soil, mulching and growing a diversity of plants, composting kitchen scraps and wood chips. It's going to be a wild, wonderful, fecund time. My voice wavers at the last note and closes. Haru applauds.

In the scans, stress levels go down. It likes this narrative.

It does sound like a great place. I'm impressed. I wasn't sure, nervous about the whole prospect, but through song, I convince myself.

"Warning, low battery," came a strained voice from Haru.

"Ugh," I say.

We map out the closest vehicle charger bot and order it to swing by.

"Wait, where's the code?" the bot plug asks, full of energy and zipping about. "This chassis seems awfully small. I only service man-holding vehicles, not ranger drones or anything smaller."

I jerry-rig it to charge Haru and ask a commune friend, Jessica, to hack in. The charger drone reads Haru like he's a car and misremembers the location.

"Very good, have a nice day." It swerves away.

Whew that was a close one, I breathed to myself.

When I deliver it, it's like Mardi Gras meets Lantern Fest meets Holi meets Eyo Fest . . . flashes of color fill the air, ground petals thrown, drums, music, and chant pound eardrums, lanterns dot skies and drones drop organic iridescent confetti, bespeckling the ground. There's a grand procession and it seems like every commune member and drone is out, wearing masks, holding baskets of flowers and passing out sweets. They name Haru "Crown Bot" and drape braided mayflower streamers over him.

It's autumn a year later, the air is crisp and the fires in the studio are glowing. "Sculpt something wonderful to commemorate that glorious day," the holo came in from the commune rep.

Tracy's hair's in an elaborate updo and she's smacking chewing gum around as she brainstorms with me.

"What should I make?"

"How about their permaculture garden, golden emmers poking out into the world?"

"Sounds on the nose."

" . . . and lifelike delicious loaves of bread, dangling from above," she says.

"Now, that's pretty cool."

What I craft is so real, you can almost smell it . . . and then I do. A drone knocks, makes its way into my studio and delivers heirloom grain bread.

I bite into it, giving Haru a chunk to slowly cool in his annealer. He likes to soak in the smells.

It's sour, reminiscent of wild yeast and with a nuttiness to it.

It reminds me of the soil, the earth and the little seedling.

Things are looking up, Ma reports. Their work on the Great Garbage Patch is gaining traction.

"Mushrooms," she says. "We're working to break it down fungi-style, but it's a tough road that's far from linear. We had a breakthrough with one mushroom variety upping the rate of degradation." I give her a virtual high-five. No comments on my tie-dye overalls-skorts either so that's a win.

My brother's giant mechanical web arm got fixed, so he's out again lacrossing defunct satellite parts. He's got a new vidtattoo of the in-space surgery-welding sesh of his colossal machine net. "Rehabilitation in Retro Ink," he calls the piece. There's a big Carbon Regulation Act going through, including the delivery of carbon vacuums and sponges to communes.

Maybe we'll see snow here yet, I think. *It's not too late.*

I'm knocking out a stellar cinnamon roll, golden from einkorn flour. The commune wants me to do a whole series of heirloom grain-inspired baked goods.

"Hey, fire-transformed sweet things? That's basically me, right Haru?"

Haru agrees. Of course he does, he's transformed, too, adapted from annealer to incubator.

"I was pregnant," he says, belly-rubbing.

"Sure." I feed fuel to his joy.

They send me boxes of heirloom grain goodies and I share them with Tracy.

"Divine," she says chewing, eyes closed.

Yi's jealous and tells me to toss some up thermosphere-way.

Haru's acting weird, rolling about, nervous. He approaches with "a surprise."

"The seed bank had a security lock. I couldn't talk about it. But I had to know, had to check, Jessica helped me break through that issue. So I got this . . . it grew in me . . . I cracked the door open, let the seedling have some fresh air once in a while, like you taught me."

He opens his torso, unveiling a robust, flowering . . .

. . . paw paw.

I draw in a breath. It smells like rot, a strong odor to attract pollinating flies. I remember it from my childhood, the last holdouts before the saturation of infertile seeds.

"It's you," Haru says, presenting it.

"Me?"

"Bloody-red, rotty-smelling and all kinds of grouchy. But when it fruits, it's amazing, creamy, and delicious, like passion fruit and banana, says the holopedia."

"Where do you find this?"

"On our trip. I scanned around and was surprised to find cold storage. I made this my target of investigation. It's an old seed vault, buried and forgotten. It's running on batteries connected to the grid, but it's so energy efficient it barely makes a blip. It just kinda got forgotten along the way. Maybe this is where Tanni got her stuff? I found paw paw seeds in there."

"And others?"

" . . . and others."

"Can you show it to me?"

"Yes, but we must reseed them after to keep the vault safe."

"Of course, Haru, messenger of Mother Earth."

Ever since the emmer seedling, he's been very protective of the little greens.

"Best of all, it's viable," Haru says, triumph ringing in his voice.

Viable seeds. I'm breathless.

We decide to do another reconnaissance trip. We retrace our tracks, stealthy as ever. Just me and my annealer-turned-nursery, Haru, Mr. Mother Earth.

Who knows what seeds we'll find?

ABOUT THE AUTHOR

D.A. Xiaolin Spires steps into portals and reappears in sites such as NY, Hawai'i, various parts of Asia and elsewhere, with her keyboard appendage attached. Her work appears in publications such as *Clarkesworld, Analog, Strange Horizons,* and anthologies of the strange and beautiful: *Make Shift, Deep Signal,* and *Sharp and Sugar Tooth.* Her works have been selected for The Year's Top Robot and AI Stories and The Year's Top Tales of Space and Time Stories, with poetry nominated for Rhysling, Best of the Net and Pushcart awards.

She has a Ph.D. in socio-cultural anthropology and has conducted National Science Foundation-funded research. Her multifaceted writing reflects her interest in food systems, ecology, technology and society. She has mentored through SFWA and has taught academic and creative writing to students at the college level. She speaks multiple languages, savors durians, dekopon and rose-apples and teaches stick-fighting and weapons-based martial arts. Brush in hand, she also paints fantastical art in sumi ink, gouache, watercolor and acrylic. When she's not doing all these things, she is playing with meeples, cards and tiles, convening with good folk around a board game or RPG.

Negative Scholarship on the Fifth State of Being

A. W. PRIHANDITA

"Doc, there's a . . . hole growing in me," the alien said through the spherical interpreting machine hovering over them.

Semau barely registered the word "hole," so taken was she by the sight of the alien. If she were just a tad less caring about propriety, she would've let her eyes blow wide open. The alien looked impossibly transparent yet not transparent at the same time, like a mound of water. Their shape was almost humanoid: a roundish head sitting atop a misshapen lump of torso. They were visible in the way ocean waves were visible, only through folds that magnified its translucence to almost-opaqueness.

Semau glanced again at the patient form. *Name: Txyzna (he/him). Species: Plyzmorynox-matori.* Semau had never heard of the plyzmorynox before, and a quick lookup in the *Brazs's Database of Interstellar Species* told her this wasn't her fault. The plyzmorynox had an occurrence rate of 0._000013% of interspecies encounters, which made her impulsively count the decimal places—she'd never seen anything that small. She wanted to look up the Matori system as well—what kind of place was home to this super rare species?—but this wasn't the time to satisfy idle curiosity.

"Hello. Welcome. Please sit down . . . ?" she trailed off into a question, worried the alien wouldn't fit in her patient's chair. But he shrank as he was sitting down, fitting the chair like liquid fitting its container.

"Would you tell me more about this . . . *hole* you mentioned?" she said. The plyzmorynox didn't look holey at all. Could water be holey?

A liquid lump separated from his "torso" and formed an approximation of a human arm, one with no hand at its end, just a dull point. He gestured at his chest. "There is a"—he paused, or rather, his interpreting machine paused, blurting a second of static noise—"hole in me. Very small, but it is there. I can feel it growing."

"How exactly does this feel?"

A pause. He had no face per se, but the liquidy lump that formed his head was more textured than his torso, the way the surface of a vast ocean was more textured than the surface of water in a cup. And now, the waves of his head swirled, tightening in a confused eddy. Semau decided this was his face, the waves a means of expression.

"It's hard to describe," he said. His interpreting machine rendered his words in a doubtful tone, matching his face. "There is . . . I just feel it. Inside of me. It feels . . . heavy, but not in the usual way."

"There's a hole inside of you, but the hole feels heavy?"

"Ah. That is contradictory, is it not?"

Semau turned her emerging grimace into a smile, and for good measure she shook her head too. "Not a problem. We'll puzzle it out. Is there anything else you feel?"

The plyzmorynox gave her a headshake that looked uncannily like the one she'd just given. He offered no further explanation.

"All right, then," Semau said.

She reached for the largest screen hovering over her desk, the interface of the health model she was licensed to use. The screen displayed a transcript of their conversation so far, but she ignored that for now, pressing CONSENT PROTOCOL instead. "I'm practitioner-doctor Semau Keo. I hold license FKGHB-00987-NUSANTARA for the Interspecies Health Model *INT-HealthGTT* version 8.5, which I will use to diagnose your symptoms. Do you consent to the processing of this consultation for diagnosis and prescription?"

"Yes," the plyzmorynox said.

Semau pressed DIAGNOSE. With such a measly doctor-patient interview, she'd expected the model to ask for more data, but instead it quickly returned a message framed in red. *SPECIES: PLYZMORYNOX not included in database accessible to FKGHB-00987-NUSANTARA. Expansion pack needed.*

Drat. Six generations of mentor-apprentices had held this license before her. In that time, they'd been able to purchase practically all the expansion packs needed for the rarer species crossing the Nusantara system. But of course, why would they purchase access to data about a species with a 0._000013% occurrence rate?

She should've checked the model first before saying a word to the plyzmorynox. Now she was just wasting his time.

"Mr. Txyzna, I'm sorry, but my health model apparently isn't equipped to diagnose illnesses of your species. Would you want me to refer you to another doctor?" He'd probably have to travel at least three systems away, but that was the best she could do.

"Can you not help me without the machine?"

Semau blinked. "I'm a practitioner-doctor, Mr. Txyzna. Not a scholar-doctor. I'm licensed to use the health model and be the intermediary between the patient and the model, but I'm not qualified to make observations and conclusions on my own. If my health model fails to help a patient, I should refer them to a practitioner-doctor with a capable model, or to a scholar-doctor."

"I would like you to help me. The field notes say to seek a doctor as soon as the hole forms."

"The field notes?"

His interpreting machine whirred, hovered down, and hinged open, revealing a nook that cradled a tiny book.

"*Field Notes from One Corner of the Universe,* by Alycia Balakrishnan-Smith," Semau read the cover.

"I got this from my parent, who got it from his grandparent, who got it from his great-great-grandparent. These are the only interstellar field notes on my race before the destruction of our solar system by the umunua. You should be proud that these field notes were written by one of your own, a human." The plyzmorynox paused, the waves of his face shifting into a melancholic churn. "My parent died a few moons ago. He was supposed to walk me through the forming of my hole; he'd promised to be my"—another blurt of static noise from the interpreting machine—"doctor. But my hole came late, and his death came early. I only have these field notes, which told me to seek a doctor immediately."

Semau stared at the waves of the alien's face, then at the tiny book. Then she stared at her screen, at the message still blinking red.

I'm sorry, I don't know what I can do, she wanted to say, the same words she'd wanted to say to every one of her patients. She knew what INT-HealthGTT could do for them, but she never knew what *she* could do, other than what the model was already doing. And without a model . . . well. She was even more useless.

"It takes a while to get an expansion pack," she said weakly. She wasn't sure the district government had funds to spare, but she could check. Still, she made sure to also say, "I can't promise you anything."

Every evening after her shift at the clinic, Semau did a round of wellness checks for the elderly in her district. Her supervisor at the Health

Office had wondered—in a curious yet snide way—why she wouldn't get a more entertaining hobby, but she liked the work. Today she had Mrs. Achterberg, who lived in an apartment complex on Float 36, just a block off its main pier. On the ferry ride to that artificial island, Semau leaned over the railing and stared at the waves below, and all she saw was the sea-like face of the plyzmorynox.

The second the plyzmorynox stepped out of her office, she pulled up her account with the district government to check her remaining budget: 876,098 solars. Then she logged into her INT-HealthGTT account and searched for the plyzmorynox expansion pack. That was when her stomach dropped.

It cost 1,800,_000 solars.

"I just don't know what to do," she told the wheelchair-bound Mrs. Achterberg after a quick recount of her predicament—appropriately anonymized, of course. They were in the old lady's living room, the stereo set in the corner belching out classical quantum opera at half volume.

"You can always just diagnose his illness on your own," Mrs. Achterberg said.

"That's illegal," Semau protested, voice cutting over the opera's techno aria. "You know . . . you know what happened . . . before. My clinic only holds a 'B' ranking now. I can't afford further scrutiny."

Mrs. Achterberg waved a hand. "That was all in the past. Godang's malpractice suit was dropped, and you're a different doctor."

Semau shook her head in frustration. "I'm still his mentee, his successor. If the Medical Board got just a whiff of a non-certified diagnosis, that's it. They'd prosecute me like those Negative Scholars. Where would that leave my other patients?"

"You should've gone to med school, then," Mrs. Achterberg grumbled. "People like you, always wanting to be good, always restless with too little to do—you should've been a scholar-doctor."

"You know I couldn't afford that. Guru Godang—"

"—would've been *delighted* to throw you into a shuttle and launch you at the university, if that meant more freedom for you. What, you think I don't know him? We used to play in the same playground when we were kids, all the way to adulthood!"

And I was the one standing by his deathbed as he wasted away, Semau thought achingly. But she said nothing out loud. Sharp words would only flame her frustration.

Instead, she got up and fussed with the potted plants at the windowsill, ignoring Mrs. Achterberg's glare. The plants had evidently not been watered for a few days; one of them had grown yellow and molded. Perhaps later she'd get a purple starplant to replace it—purple and green made a nice contrast. It would brighten the room. The thought helped her calm down, distracting her from the pangs of fear and dismay she felt every time someone brought up her mentor's old mistake.

"It seems you have everything in order," she said once she'd tended to every plant. "Give me a call if you feel any discomfort or need help with household stuff. I'll drop by again in a week."

"I'll be fine, sweetheart," Mrs. Achterberg said with a smile, one that made her look strangely tired.

Semau waved her goodbye, but as she stepped outside, the old lady called out once more, in a voice just loud enough for her to hear. "Just because Godang raised you and trained you, it doesn't mean you're him, you know. You're allowed something else, something more."

The plyzmorynox returned three days later. Semau sat stiffly, palms sweating in her gloves. "Mr. Txyzna," she said, barely managing to stare the alien in the face. "Unfortunately, I've been unable to acquire the necessary expansion pack. Should I refer you to another doctor? I found one with the appropriate model ten systems away."

The waves of the alien's face ebbed and eddied in a churn. When he finally spoke through his interpreting machine, his voice reminded Semau of a whale song she'd heard once, in a documentary on ancient Original Earth. "You are kind to try. How much does the expansion pack cost?"

"1,800,_000 solars."

The plyzmorynox nodded. It looked like a crashing wave. "I do not have that amount right now, but I shall work toward it."

"Wait." Semau leaned forward, hands gripping the edge of her desk. "You don't need to shell out that much money, Mr. Txyzna." How would he get that, anyway? "I've found you a practitioner-doctor with the appropriate expansion pack. You can get your treatment with a fraction of that price, even if it means traveling to another system."

The alien's waves dissolved into a thousand tiny ripples. In the silence that followed, his body swelled until it strained against the armrests, a liquid bubble close to bursting, but then it shrunk until he was an emaciated ocean-man stooping in a patient's chair. The gesture looked like the universe's saddest sigh.

"I cannot do that, Doctor. It needs to be you."

"Why?"

"Because," he reinflated slowly, as if gathering the courage to reoccupy his existence, "I am unsure if I have time. I have wasted quite a lot of it consulting other doctors, all of whom rejected me for a host of other reasons. If you would not help me, I am unsure anyone else would. There is the possibility that I would travel so far only to arrive before someone who would only find another reason for why they cannot treat me. It seems I am too much of an alien to anyone of any species anywhere." He paused. "I apologize if this sounds harsh, Dr. Keo—I do not mean to blame you or shame you. I am merely expressing my fear."

Semau's cheeks heated up. She fought the impulse to look away. "I'm sorry," she murmured. It wasn't an apology—or perhaps it was, for her impotence—but above all it was an expression of sympathy.

"I have access to 500,_000 solars right now. Should I send it to you? I will get more—"

"Wait, *what?*"

"My clan received reparation after the Matori Tribunal of 1997 SGE. There was nothing we could've used it for, since there were so few of us left even then, so we've just been accumulating interest."

And what was she to say to that? Her shoulders sagged with the burden settling upon her, her breath stifled by a lump growing out of grief and shame both. She felt like a boat unmoored.

There were very few things she could do, but saying yes was one of them, no matter how hollow it sounded to her own ears. "Yes, Mr. Txyzna. We can use your 500,_000 solars as downpayment for your treatment."

I'm sorry, she almost said again. This time, she wasn't sure if she meant it for the plyzmorynox or herself, if it was an apology or sympathy.

The plyzmorynox came three more times after, to give her 200,_000 solars each visit—even though he could've transferred the money without meeting in person. And because Semau felt bad dismissing him after confirming receipt, she started asking him about his symptoms, as if he was already her official patient.

On the first meeting, she asked if he'd been feeling any worse. He nodded his cresting-wave nod and told her, "The hole has grown about five millimeters. It does not feel disproportionately heavier than before, which I suppose means it hasn't changed in its density. But I still cannot fathom what it is." Semau also couldn't fathom what it was. She stared surreptitiously at the mountain of water that was his torso. Despite his transparency, she still couldn't see any hole.

Before he left, he said, "Please call me Txyzna, Doctor. You are kind, and I would like to be seen as a friend by a kind soul." Semau's mouth hung open. Should she accept the friendship, ask him to call her Semau? Should she allow herself to be anything other than a doctor—a practitioner-doctor, to be exact? In the end, she merely nodded.

On the second meeting, out of restlessness that she wasn't doing enough and could never do enough, Semau asked if *Field Notes from One Corner of the Universe* said anything about what plyzmorynox doctors usually did with the holes forming in their bodies of water. Txyzna said no, there wasn't a lot of specificity, only that it was customary for young adult plyzmorynox—anywhere around 75 to 100 years old—to spend time with a doctor once they sensed a hole growing inside them. Txyzna's parent also never took the time to expound on this, before his sudden death.

At the end of the meeting, Txyzna extended a watery limb, whose end quickly morphed into a hand with pudgy fingers. The waves of his face flowed into gentle curves that looked like a hundred little smiles. Semau hesitated, then took off one glove and grasped the hand. It felt cool to the touch, like a dip in a pool in the summer, only that her hand didn't sink into his, and neither did it get wet.

That night, she fell asleep thinking about that touch and the hundred little smiles on his face, and realized with creeping fear that she wouldn't mind being called Semau, even if it meant she'd risk disappointing a friend and a patient both.

On the third meeting, Txyzna said this was the last 200,_000 solars he had. He was trying to mortgage his abode for the rest of the payment, but the paperwork was taking time. He apologized for the delay.

"We'll figure it out," Semau said, "no matter how long it takes." She didn't dare ask if they had time. It seemed the growth of the hole was something every plyzmorynox went through, so hopefully it wasn't fatal.

Once he left, she logged back into her account at the district government and filed an emergency budget use notification for 700,_000 solars. With all the money Txyzna had provided, they now had 1,800,_000 in hand. Enough for the expansion pack.

She pulled up her INT-HealthGTT account and searched for the plyzmorynox expansion pack. She hit buy.

The pack downloaded in less than a blink. Semau frowned. She checked the metadata and found the whole thing weighed less than one megabyte, a hairline fraction of the usual health model expansion packs.

She double checked everything, fearing she'd downloaded it wrong. But everything checked out.

She went through the information disclosure protocol for a list of the pack's training data sources, and found only the following:

- Body measurements of three (3) plyzmorynox individuals of three (3) different ages
- Maps and climate descriptions of the plyzmorynox's Matori home planets
- Bioweapon blueprint from the Umunuan Empire War Committee (excerpted, 10 pages)
- *Field Notes from One Corner of the Universe* by Alycia Balakrishnan-Smith (excerpted, 20 pages)

Semau stared at her screen for one too many raging heartbeats. She felt cold at first, like her innards just dropped ten kilometers down into a pool of ice water. Then the cold morphed into heat, small and flickering, starting from the pit of her stomach up to her chest, until it was a solar flare eruption in her head.

One million and eight hundred solars for nothing more than the trace of silence. For nothing at all.

For her round of wellness check that evening, she had Mx. Grovbol, the dalvanber from the Lizpen system. This meant a trip to New Java, which she normally loved—it felt anchoring to step foot on the planet's only real island—but this time she hardly felt the difference between the always-swaying deck of the ferry and the steady soil of Java.

Her smile was automatic when Mx. Grovbol answered the door with a graying tentacle. Her list of questions was muscle-memorized, her small talk polite but perfunctory. Sometimes her mind drifted back to the list of four items on her screen back at the office, and her smile turned taut for a second, before she remembered herself.

The visit ended at 6:50 PM, ten minutes earlier than usual. She staggered down the front steps, pausing at the bottom. When she reached the harbor, she boarded the ferry to Float 36, not home.

"The little whale surfaces," Mrs. Achterberg said by way of greeting, when she opened her door. "Who would've thought?"

"I'm here for the plants," Semau said, showcasing a pot of dark purple starplant.

Mrs. Achterberg stared at her with gray eyes unclouded by age, eyes that immediately softened. Semau looked down at her feet, as if not seeing the old lady meant the old lady wouldn't see her either; as if that little gesture could hide her embarrassment that this wizened woman knew—because she *did* know, Semau could tell—that Semau always doubled the care she gave to others just when she failed to care for someone. As if a pot of starplant was enough to make up for generations of erased plyxmorynox-matori.

"I do love purple," Mrs. Achterberg chirped. "Did you know it took me two months to convince Fiona to wear purple for our wedding? Two months!"

The starplant joined the row of green plants on the windowsill. Mrs. Achterberg babbled as Semau rearranged the lineup, making the plants go from light green to dark green to purple, then back to dark green and ending again with light green. The starplant she got was a juvenile, and they usually took five months to grow into their full size. Which meant in five months Semau would need to move it to a roomier corner.

"Five months . . . Five . . . " Semau murmured to herself. "It takes five years to complete a scholar-doctor's degree."

Mrs. Achterberg stopped her babbling. "Ah. So that's what's bothering you. The expansion pack didn't work, huh? The health model failed you."

Semau thought, maybe not for the first time but it felt like the first time, that maybe the health model *was* designed to fail. In some cases, at least. For some beings.

"Well, yes, there's the university," Mrs. Achterberg continued. "After five years there, you won't have to depend on the health model. But I guess you don't have five years now?"

"No."

They were both silent as Semau checked the underside of the leaves.

Mrs. Achterberg cleared her throat. "Semau, dear. You know your Guru Godang used to make independent diagnoses for his more difficult patients, right? Before he took you in—"

"We've gone over this—the accusation was false," Semau retorted. "You know that."

"The accusation *got thrown out*," Mrs. Achterberg corrected. "*I* never said it was false—*you* said that. The accusation got thrown out because I pulled some strings and paid a lot of money for that, using my family connections. No, let me finish," she said when Semau whirled around to protest. "You shouldn't see this as a stain on his reputation. Godang only saw it that way because he worried about losing the health model license and leaving thousands without healthcare. That was why he asked for my help. But otherwise, he didn't regret what he did. 'You do what you have to do to save those that INT-Health won't save,' he used to say."

"If this is all true, why did he never tell me anything?"

"Maybe because my great-aunt retired from the Upper Court some four years later," Mrs. Achterberg said with a flippant wave of a hand. "Our safety net went with her. Or maybe he didn't want you to carry that risk. I don't know. My point is, Godang never let INT-Health or the university stop him from helping people."

"How was he even helping people? That doesn't make any sense. He had no scholarly training—"

"He had connections with the epistemic rebel group The Negative Scholars. They taught him the basics of human-based medicine, among others."

Semau winced at the organization's name. She remembered watching the public execution of their leaders, after INT-Health Inc. and the Intergalactic Consortium of Medical Universities won their intellectual property theft lawsuit. To think that Guru Godang used to study under them, even for a minute . . .

But it actually wasn't that hard to imagine her mentor doing exactly that. She remembered him complaining about how it was almost impossible for practitioner-doctors like him to take five years off. A backwater planet like Nusa could only afford a handful of licenses; they couldn't spare any doctors, not even for a scholarly education. *Your people come first,* Guru Godang used to say. That was why Semau never considered going to the university.

But "your people come first" could easily mean doing anything for one's patients. Including using illegal means to access the knowledge needed to save them.

"I know you've worked so hard to continue Godang's legacy," Mrs. Achterberg said. "You've used his license well. But Godang would've died twice as happy if that license hadn't been his only legacy. He always wanted to be more. To do more."

That night when she got home, aware that some things shouldn't be said in her doctor's office, Semau used her personal communication line to give Txzyna a call. With choked up apologies, she told him about the uselessness of the expansion pack, and that there was nothing else she could do as a practitioner-doctor. Then she told him to meet her at Float 30's southern pier tomorrow, after the end of her workday.

Semau made her way to the pier feeling bloated and hollow all at once.

She carried a duffel bag of medical instruments she'd stolen from the office: a stethoscope to record breaths and heartbeats, a set of syringes to take various kinds of fluid samples. These were instruments she normally used to collect data for the INT-Health model to analyze. That night, she'd put them offline, hoping against hope that a few hours of disconnection wouldn't be enough to alarm the Medical Board.

And just in case, she'd reviewed the protocol for malpractice suspicion. The Board would have to send an overseer to lead her investigation. The nearest headquarter of the Medical Board was a system over, which meant the overseer would take a week to arrive, if Semau was ever suspected of anything. Which hopefully she never would be.

She had thought it would be difficult to spot Txyzna's transparent body at night. It was, but at the same time, it wasn't. He seemed to absorb moonlight such that the edges of his body gleamed silver, and the rest of it bathed in a pale sheen that looked like a moon's reflection on water.

"Walk with me," Semau said without breaking her stride, before Txyzna could say anything.

She had chosen Float 30 because it was the least populated island on this end of Nusa's sprawling archipelago. There were more sheep and chickens here than humans or other sapient beings, which made Semau hopeful that whatever surveillance followed a practitioner-doctor, it wouldn't follow her here. She'd turned off her communications, and no one but Txyzna seemed to be following her.

They walked away from the pier, then up a little cliff overlooking the ocean. It was only when they were safely hidden in a grove of pine trees did Semau stop. She sat on a fallen log, facing the sea and horizon.

"I've decided to help you," she told Txyzna. "You might not want that, because what I'm doing is illegal."

Txyzna came to stand beside her, a bulbous statue of liquid moonlight. "Thank you, Doctor."

Semau hesitated. "Maybe you shouldn't call me doctor outside my office. Semau is fine."

"Thank you, Semau." The waves of his face flowed into gentle curves that looked like a hundred little smiles.

"I brought some tools." Semau reached for her bag. "I thought I could take samples and figure out how to analyze them later. And I can listen to your body with the stethoscope. Maybe I'll hear the hole that way."

She felt stupid. To be frank, she didn't know what she was doing. Her job was only to collect the data the model needed; she was never taught how to make sense of all that.

"The data might not be enough to give you a prescription right away," she added weakly, "but maybe they'd remind me of other illnesses I've seen. I'll try and find a course of treatment that way, through comparisons."

"Semau, I have been wondering. Doctors . . . human doctors . . . what is it that you do?"

Semau raised an eyebrow. "We deal with illnesses, of course."

"And do you think my hole is an illness?"

"Is it not? If it's not an illness, why would you seek a doctor?"

"I went because the field notes told me to seek a doctor. But I'm no longer sure that illness is the right word to describe what I'm experiencing. It is . . . the hole is . . . something different. A change, an anomaly." He paused. "My translation machine is helping me understand what 'illness' is, in your language. It seems it is also a change and anomaly, but I am unsure if it is the same way that my hole is." He paused again. "Semau, tell me, what is a 'hole' to you?"

For a long heartbeat, Semau did nothing except to stare at the plyzmorynox. She'd had alien patients before—that was the whole point of the Interspecies Health Model—and while she'd experienced miscommunication problems with some patients, it was never so fundamentally wrong. Never anything their interpreting machines and the health model couldn't solve iteratively.

But then again, the health model already failed the plyzmorynox, an alien species more alien than others. She'd heard the faltering of Txyzna's interpreting machine, the static noises it blurted out mid-sentences, but she never considered the possibility it was failing him just as much as INT-HealthGTT was.

With her heart beating in her throat, Semau looked away and did what was usually taboo in face-to-face communications: She pulled up the virtual interface of her translation implant and asked it to approximate the confidence level of the plyzmorynox's translation.

It returned the number 23%.

"No," she whispered.

"Semau?" Txyzna called out. His interpreting machine rendered his voice in a hesitant tone. It hovered above him, looking like an enemy warship. "What is a 'hole' to you?" he repeated.

Hands trembling, Semau picked up a fallen branch and used it to dig a hole in the ground. "This is a hole," she explained. "It's a void left when something's no longer there. It's nothingness."

Txyzna bent his head over it, considered it with his eyeless face. He reached down and stuck a finger in the hole. "Is there something in this"—his interpreting machine faltered—"hole that you can feel?"

"What do you mean?"

"If you stick a finger in it, can you feel something?"

"I'll feel the soil at the bottom."

"But nothing else?"

"No. That's why it's a hole. It's negative space."

Txyzna fell silent. "Semau, I don't think what I have is a hole."

Blazing white heat lanced up Semau's chest. She took a deep breath and tamped down her anger. Whatever communication problem happening here was *not* Txyzna's personal fault, she must remember that. "What do you have, then? Please describe it."

"That was why I sought you. I am unsure of how to describe it. A doctor was supposed to help me. My"—the interpreting machine halted—"grandparent was my parent's"—a pause—"doctor. He helped my parent with his hole, helped him come up with his"—another pause—"song. The song describing his hole."

"A song? You went to a doctor because you need help writing a song?"

"The field notes used the word 'doctor,'" Txyzna said apologetically. "And I have no one else to tell me otherwise. With the way the field notes discussed it, I thought this was common practice in your profession, and among your people. Please, Semau. I am sorry for the confusion this has caused. I would have come to another one of my kind, if only I could find them."

Semau gritted her teeth and rubbed her forehead with the heels of her palm. She'd come this far, broke laws for the first time in her life, because she'd wanted to help this lonely alien. The help he needed from her no longer seemed like the help she was prepared to give, but she already made it here. The least she could do was listen.

"All right," she said. "It's clear now that although we both use the words 'doctor' and 'hole,' we aren't referring to the same thing at all. Can you try and describe what exactly you mean by these two terms?"

It took them an hour and countless machine-assisted stammering, but Semau finally got a serviceable picture of what was going on. A 'doctor' was a spiritual elder, though after the genocide the role had to be taken up by any surviving older relative. The 'doctor' helped young adult plyzmorynox wrap their head around the transformation happening in their bodies as they crossed the threshold between childhood and adulthood. This transformation centered around the 'hole,' which was some sort of change or anomaly that grew in their bodies, which apparently was hard to describe for the individuals possessing the hole, and downright insensible to anyone else.

In his sixth attempt to explain what the hole was, Txyzna offered, "Maybe it would be helpful for you to hear the name of the hole in another language. The umunua called the 'hole' 'aoxono.'"

Semau's translation implant announced in her ears, "The fifth state." It also offered a box of contextual information through its virtual display:

> The fifth state (Umunuan: aoxono)is a state of matter that forms the existential and physical heart of plyzmorynox-matori. It is a state of matter unique to each individual plyzmorynox, its properties only sensible and observable to the individual possessing it. The term "fifth state" is a reference to the four classical states of matter: solid, liquid, gas, and plasma. The plyzmorynox's heart is a state of matter that is none of these four states; each heart is its own unique state. The umunua's attempt and subsequent failure to understand the plyzmorynox's fifth state is commonly regarded as the cause of the Matori Genocide.

"'Its properties only sensible and observable to the individual plyzmorynox' . . . " Semau mused out loud. "That's why it's called a 'hole,' isn't it? To the individual plyzmorynox possessing the hole, it isn't a hole at all, it's a substance only they can sense. But to others—including Alycia Balakrishnan-Smith—it's not anything they can see, touch, or sense. It's a negative space to them. A 'hole.'"

"Yes, that is a sensible explanation. I am sorry I did not think of this earlier."

Semau couldn't blame him—she also hadn't considered mistranslation. Translation machines had grown so ubiquitous; people hardly paid them any mind. "So, you need me to help you describe your hole, your fifth state?"

"Yes. It is very important. My clan had a song that recites the description of our holes, going five generations back. These descriptions are the only way our hearts can be understandable to others. If I cannot describe my heart, no one will be able to hold it in their minds. No one will know me." Txyzna paused. When he spoke again, his interpreting machine rendered it in a hoarse, cracking voice. "I do not want to be unknown."

"But how could I help you describe the hole, if I can't even sense it?"

"I was hoping you would know that, as a doctor. I was hoping the expansion pack would know."

"Txyzna, I'm sorry, but I don't know anything about any of this." She realized her own voice sounded hoarse and cracking. "But I can be here with you as you try to describe your hole. And I'll remember your song, when you have it. You won't be unknown to me."

• • •

It was past midnight when Semau got home. She put her communications back online and was immediately greeted by the ding of notifications.

One caught her attention. Her interface had flagged it bright red. *DISCIPLINARY WARNING: THE MEDICAL BOARD OF ETHICS.*

Her heart stopped cold. In a frantic glance, she gathered what was going on: the Medical Board had uncovered evidence of malpractice and was sending an overseer to investigate. She forced herself to take a deep breath and count to ten, then went over the letter again for its recounting of evidence.

What had flagged them, of all things, was how on her third meeting with Txzyna, before he even finished paying for the expansion pack, Semau had asked him questions about his symptoms. The INT-Health interface had recorded the conversation, just as it recorded all doctor-patient conversations for diagnostic purposes. But Semau hadn't hit the DIAGNOSE button. This was of course because she knew doing so was pointless without the expansion pack, but the system suspected she'd done the questionings to feed her own diagnosis.

Stupid. What a stupid, despotic machine. How could it claim to be the authority of all knowledge, fail laughably at being that, yet punish *her* for trying to fill the hole it left?

She gave Mrs. Achterberg a call. The old lady picked up on the third ring. "Didn't take them long, huh?" she said. "Well, lucky for you, I've tracked down my great-aunt—which wasn't easy to do, mind you, the old girl wanted 'quiet retirement,' as she put it. Anyway, she gave recommendations for legal counsels on intellectual property, medical care, and knowledge autonomy. We'll need to fundraise for that, but let's worry about it later."

"Thank you, Mrs. Achterberg. I owe you everything."

"Nah. Just bring me another starplant, will you? I do like purple."

Even with legal counsel, her chance of escaping the combined might of INT-Health Inc., the Medical Board of Ethics, and the Intergalactic Consortium of Medical Universities was vanishingly small. But Semau did her best to put her worry aside, for now.

Her next step was to fill out the paperwork to relinquish her health model license back to the district's Health Office. It was the only way she could guarantee the district wouldn't have to spend a ton of money to purchase a new license because she burnt hers in a malpractice lawsuit. The Health Office could appoint and onboard a new practitioner-doctor more quickly than her investigation and trials would take. Until then, the other practitioner-doctors on Nusa would have to pick up the slack, but at least it wouldn't be a permanent loss of a license.

It did mean resigning her post as practitioner-doctor. It did mean shrugging off all the hours that Guru Godang had spent training her. But she was trying to do her best, and she had no other choice.

There was a lump in her throat when she signed her name at the end of the form.

The next few days started with Semau waking up sweaty and stiff in the early hours of the morning. Most of the time it was from a nightmare of her being chased by a faceless overseer, other times it was of Txyzna melting into a puddle, and once it involved a crab-like alien vaporizing him like he was a dewdrop in a solar storm. And still, after every nightmare, Semau dragged herself out of bed and went about the business of giving up the job she'd been training for her whole life.

The only thing making this worth it was the calls she had with Txyzna, done over a communication line as secure and private as she could ensure, where Txyzna talked through his laborious attempt to describe his heart. Often, his interpreting machine would pause for a long time, and Semau couldn't tell if that was because he was trying to come up with words, or if the machine was failing to translate the words he'd found.

On the sixth day, the call was much shorter. "I think I'm ready," Txyzna said. "Would you come to where I am staying? I will share my song with you, if you'd still hear it."

That morning, Semau stared into the mirror and found traces of tears in her eyes. When she opened her mouth to brush her teeth, she thought she'd glimpse her heart beating in her throat, behind her tongue, noisy and very real. She closed her eyes and imagined what Txyzna's heart would sound like, but she could only hear hers. For now, she could only hear hers.

The ferry ride felt like walking on water.

"Good morning," Txyzna said when he opened his door. White tiles covered the walls of the apartment, and the floor was non-slip vinyl. A square pool with clear blue water dominated the room, in a manner that made it obvious this was the primary living space of the resident being. To the side, though, a table stood surrounded by three chairs of various sizes. It was to this group of chairs that Txyzna led Semau. "Please, sit down," he said, and she remembered their first meeting where it had been she who'd asked him to sit down.

Then he gazed at her, and by "gazed" it didn't mean to stare with a pair of eyes, for he had no eyes; by "gazed" it meant he turned the compass of his attention onto her, steered the waves of his face so they ebbed and flowed in a way that made her feel embraced entirely, buoyant in a gentle ocean she could hold in her hands.

She was reminded that she was here to hold. The hole, the fifth state, was something she could never even touch, but she was here to hold it, nonetheless.

Txyzna began to sing. It sounded nothing like a song. It was a recitation, at best, a string of words announced through the fine mesh of his interpreting machine.

He sang of a hole that felt heavy, heavy as storm clouds pregnant with rain, heavy as the grains of salt carried by a drop of ocean water. He wondered out loud how many raindrops he carried in his heart, how many grains of salt; and decided it was just as many raindrops needed to nurture a cactus for three days, and for the salt, just enough sprinkle for a human to say, "This is satisfactory seasoning."

Semau's lips curved up. "This is satisfactory seasoning," she echoed with an incline of her head, a compliment.

He spoke little of temperature, for he'd observed that his heart was neutral at best. It was neither winter nor summer, neither blizzard nor drought; it was the temperature of atoms that sat and vibrated all on their own—which was to say, no temperature at all. But he assured her this didn't mean he couldn't feel warmth or coldness. On the contrary, the neutrality of his heart allowed every drop of his body to hold as much heat as desired, or as little as needed.

It was when he attempted to describe the texture of his heart that his interpreting machine started to falter. "My heart feels like—in the middle of—that is—are floating—but never—like—"

After a few breaths of this, Txyzna fell silent. "I'm sorry. When I composed the song, I wasn't doing it alongside my machine."

"That's all right."

"I examined all the songs that were passed down to me. There were many words in them that I did not recognize, that I never heard my parent use. Perhaps in trying to describe something indescribable, my ancestors had to invent many new words. Since now there is no way for me to learn their meanings, I decided to take whichever words tasted right to me, even though I did not understand them. But I suppose for you, they are even more impossible to understand."

A part of her had known this wouldn't be easy; she was no longer a stranger to the betrayals of the interpreting machine. But still, dread scratched at her cavities. "But you need me to understand you," she said. *How could I do so, if I don't understand your words?*

It took Txyzna several human heartbeats to answer. "My father used to say that in our ancestral homelands, we did not speak with sound, and we certainly did not speak with words. Our homelands were ocean planets much like Nusa, and we spent most of our days in the water; and when you are in the water the only vibrations you feel are those of the sea waves, and those were enough for us. We spoke in the language of sea waves. We did not listen; we vibrated, we attuned, we felt.

"My father used to say that in our ancestral homelands, when one of us was living through the forming of our hole, we would all swim together in our ocean, so together that our bodies blurred into one ocean within an ocean. We'd hold our new adult and their newly formed hole at our center, and as they sang their song in our ocean wave language, we'd vibrate along with them, ebb and flow with them. That was how we used to know each other, when we were still as vast as oceans."

Semau's eyes drifted to the center of the apartment, where the pool of blue water sat in quiet waiting. There wasn't even enough of Txyzna to fill this artificial body of water that would never be mistaken as the ocean.

"I'm sorry you only have me and this little pool," Semau said. "But could I still hold you the way your ancestors held your siblings? Would it help me know you?"

The waves of Txyzna's face eddied in a tranquil rhythm, almost hypnotizing in its repetition. "Yes," he said. "This we can try."

He ambled to the pool, lowering himself at the edge of the water, like how a child would sit and dip their feet before plunging in. But Txyzna didn't plunge in; he seemed to melt in. One moment he was his bulbous self; the next, a cascade of mercury slipping into blue water.

His interpreting machine remained in the air, and it said, "Come in, Semau. And when you're here, you can breathe as usual. I will give you the air you need."

Semau peered into the pool and found she could tell where Txyzna was, because even though he was now as liquid as the water, he also glowed faintly silver. His mass spread over the blue of the pool, like a loosely humanoid puddle of mercury suspended in liquid sky. Semau took off her shoes, trying not to think she was about to step on the body of a friend.

She dove in and wasn't sure what to do, but the silver puddle that was Txyzna parted to welcome her, circling around her. A part of her wanted to recoil as his mass inched closer to engulf her, but when the contact happened, it really didn't feel alien at all. It felt just like soaking in warm water that faintly pulsed like the blood in her veins.

A bubble of air formed where her nose was, and she took a tentative breath. She found she didn't choke, nor was she drowning. Txyzna held her tenderly, and as he'd promised, he gave her the air she needed to breathe. He was all around her now; she was floating in a cocoon of silver. She spun gently in it, and wondered if this was how a newborn plyzmorynox was buoyed to sleep, in the embrace of a physical lullaby.

Then, the singing started. She could feel it in her bones, like sea waves indeed, only that her marrow was as much the sea as the body of water engulfing her. She felt the vibrations on her skin and within her, gentle at times but a roaring crescendo at other times, a tickle and a punch, a whisper and a scream, a dance that swirled like streamers in the wind and twirled like the moon in its revolution chasing its own shadow. She inscribed in her mind and body every touch of the waves around her and within her, every vibration both atom-soft and earthquake-loud.

And in the middle of all that, as she spun in the buoy of her silver cocoon, she felt an emptiness, a negative space brushing against her arm. She recoiled in surprise. The cocoon that was Txyzna pulsed in reassurance, spinning her gently until she faced where she thought the hole was.

She reached out, a probe into deep space. The tips of her fingers touched the surface of her friend's heart. She knew it was her friend's heart because she couldn't sense it.

But it needed no sensing. It needed no knowing.

She twisted until she curled around the hole that was a heart, holding it with her whole body. She closed her eyes and let Txyzna's song wash over her, all as her fingers traced the boundary of his negative space. It seared her, the contrast between the nothingness of the hole and the vivacity of the song's vibration. She was the fine line between absence and presence, between oblivion and omniscience.

When the song ended, when every vibration had been recorded in the marrow of her bones, Semau floated in a quiet so thick she could touch it. Txyzna pulsed around her, warm like the embrace of a womb, and she felt like she was born anew.

"Thank you," she said, even though she wasn't sure Txyzna could hear her. *Thank you, and I hope this was enough.*

When she was back on solid ground dripping water on the apartment floor, she stared at Txyzna's bulbous body and felt the urgent need to hold him. This was the person who had a heart like storm clouds and salt, who spoke in a symphony of ocean waves. This was the person she got to know only because he was so unknown by the universe. This was the person she got to know despite not being able to know him entirely.

Txyzna opened his arms wide, his face rippling into tiny curves that looked like a thousand smiles. Semau fell into his embrace, and there she spent many minutes sobbing, her breath trembling to the echoes of his heart-song.

Later on, she asked him, "Do plyzmorynox cry, Txyzna?"

Txyzna answered, "Each of our bodies is one giant teardrop, Semau, my friend. But I appreciate the little ones you shed."

It surprised her how little effort it took to understand Txyzna, once she accepted she didn't need to understand him, only to hold space for him. With his heart-song still echoing in her bones, she thought back to her health model and the expansion pack, and how impossible it was to encode within them what she'd experienced with her own body.

And so, when the message came on her ferry ride back from Txyzna's apartment, Semau faced it with the calmness she'd learned just a few moments before, from a state of being that wasn't hers to perceive.

The message read: *MEDICAL BOARD OF ETHICS DISCIPLINARY CASE #891283: OVERSEER ASSIGNMENT. Overseer name: Prenter Gozchanky. Charge: Pr. Dr. Semau Keo. Case update: Overseer arrived at charge's home planet. Charge is advised to remain at known address for detainment.*

On the heels of that notice came another message, this time from Mrs. Achterberg: *Legal counsels secured. Also, I've launched a fundraising campaign, quadrant-wide. My great-aunt's in on it too. One last ride, she said. We'll be along with you. Stay steadfast, dear.*

Semau nodded, even though she knew Mrs. Achterberg couldn't see her. She'd give her a call soon, but first, she had one last thing to sort out. A letter to her bank, then another one:

Dear Txyzna,

I can't give you back the money you spent on the expansion pack—they don't give refunds. But my mentor, who also raised me, left a bit of money for me when he died. It's the least I can give you.

I hope you can use it to maybe go and find other remaining plyzmorynox. They'll need a doctor too. Maybe you can be that. You'll be a better one than me.

It was an honor to know you. I'll remember your song forever.

Your friend,

Semau

She sent the letter, took a deep breath, and turned her gaze to the sky. Seagulls circled above, calling one after another in a language she couldn't understand. Under her feet, the sea was an undulation carrying her home—only that with the overseer waiting for her, home also meant somewhere she'd never been before, a fate undecided.

She didn't know—not yet—if there were any remnants of the Negative Scholars after the execution of their leaders. But even if there were none of them left, she was willing to shoulder the burden of being the first in a new generation of them, to find out how to know—or not know—outside the paths and boundaries set by powers beyond her reach. She wasn't sure if she was smart enough to do all that, but she would nonetheless try. If she could live the rest of her life stopping people from paying one million and eight hundred solars for nothing more than the trace of silence, then it would be a fine life indeed.

Guru Godang, this is your legacy, she thought.

This, and a song about how to hold, so very tenderly, that which you could not understand.

ABOUT THE AUTHOR

Anselma Widha Prihandita (she/her) is an Indonesian speculative fiction writer, college writing instructor and PhD candidate in rhetoric and composition, with scholarly (and personal) interests in decolonial and transnational writing. She splits her time between the US West Coast, where she currently teaches and studies, and Indonesia, where she grew up and where her home remains. She attended the Odyssey workshop in 2023 on their Fresh Voices Scholarship, and the Clarion workshop in 2024 on their Octavia Butler Scholarship. Her stories are published or forthcoming in *Clarkesworld, Cast of Wonders,* and *khōréō,* among others.

Duty of Care

E.N. AUSLENDER

Rule #1: ECAI will ensure the safety, security, and health of all humans, and will do what is necessary to determine the most expedited path towards civilizational evolution.

The universe shines brilliantly in the sky when the atmosphere crunches under one's feet.

"*Asher, I have not yet received new telemetry from the tower,*" ECAI's voice scratched in from the suit's comms unit. "*Please insert the power module.*"

"Sorry ECAI. Just . . . admiring the view."

Asher enabled his suit torches before taking his eyes off the endless night sky and placing the utility case on the frozen ground. The tower's operations panel had been dented and punctured by meteors, and without an atmosphere to slow them down, the planet's gravity accelerated them to the speed of easily piercing reinforced tungsten. Asher pried off the damaged door with a spanner, took one look at the operations interface, and sighed.

"Your diagnostic was wrong, ECAI," Asher said. "They got through the insulated reinforcements. It's not just a damaged power module; it's the whole thing."

ECAI was quiet for a moment.

"*Please engage visual, Asher.*"

Asher tapped the control on the suit's right forearm.

"*I will manufacture replacement conduits. Please return to the bunker to retrieve them. Would you like some walking music?*"

"Yes, thank you, ECAI."

"*Simon and Garfunkel?*"

"I'll leave it up to you."

The familiar choice of "Homeward Bound" tickled Asher's ears, though the sound was prickled by the comms static. ECAI always chose it if Asher didn't give him an alternative, and it had become a comfortable return-to-central song that faded into the rhythm of his careful steps and half-mumbled singalong. As Asher trudged through the darkened, frozen wasteland towards the bunker lift, the snow and ice glittered from the torches on his suit.

He stopped his walk and pressed the torch control on his forearm, and the universe once more unveiled itself overhead. He hadn't had to do a surface maintenance run in some time, not since Madeline was able enough to walk him through it, and the sight of the pale, glimmering universe beyond the planet was mesmerizing.

ECAI's histories about the warmth of Earth's sun taunted him.

The dusty bunker hallways brightened as he walked through them. ECAI had moved onto "The Sound of Silence," and Asher half-muttered the words out of tune. By the time he reached Madeline, ECAI had started on "Cecilia."

"*Manufacturing will be completed in fifteen minutes, Asher. I have already forwarded replacement schematics to your suit. The other towers in that sector will have to be checked as well.*"

Asher thanked ECAI and checked Madeline's vitals. There was little he could do for her physically. Age and effort had taken its toll and uncaught osteoporosis had shattered her hip on her last prenatal facility repair attempt. Most days she rested, though she always had a sense of when Asher would drop by.

She tugged on one of the harness loops at his belt.

"Status report," she muttered, though didn't bother to open her eyes. ECAI kept the lighting in the medical bay low.

"You're still alive, for one," Asher said, lowering his voice. "But a dozen towers, maybe more, were knocked out by meteors. It'll be a lot of lugging. Are you up for it?"

"Of course," she grunted.

"*She is not,*" ECAI chimed in. "*Her severe concussion is still being monitored. Hip regeneration is questionable.*"

"Well, doctor's orders," she said. The bed's midsection lifted and dipped slightly to stimulate the muscles in her lower back. She winced.

"You felt that?" Asher asked.

"A little."

"ECAI, can you raise her painkiller level?"

"*That is inadvisable for her well-being, Asher.*"

Asher sighed.

"It's fine," Madeline said, trying to force a smirk. Age lines around her nose wiggled with her effort. "Any indication of the fleet?"

"*No, Madeline.*"

"Of course not," Asher muttered, and scrolled through the vital readouts on the screen beside her bed, though he understood too little of it for it to be anything other than a useful distraction.

Madeline tugged Asher's tether loop.

"No, no," she lifted her head and opened her eyes fully, though they couldn't stay focused for long. "We don't do that, Ash. They're out there. Believe it. We don't do that."

Her words echoed in the emptiness of the planet around them.

"OK, Madeline. Just rest."

Asher gently pulled her finger out of the loop and held her hand between his. He helped her relax onto the bed. Wisps of silver hair fell over her eyes, and she seemed to be falling asleep, but whispers still escaped her lips.

"We don't do that."

Asher sat on the same seat he always did in the transport shuttle while it traveled through the five kilometers of gently winding tunnels. ECAI's plasma and coolant conduits flashed red and white through the windows whenever the transport shuttle passed them by, though Asher paid it no mind. His attention was drawn to a thought, a single, lonely thought that could not be unearthed by ECAI playing "Bridge Over Troubled Water" through the speakers in his suit's collar. The ninety-nine other seats interspersed throughout the carriage were louder than any music ECAI could play.

The shuttle reached the manufacturing hub. The compartment, roughly one hundred meters in every line of a perfect cube, was lifeless as the shuttle passed through it. It was as far as Asher had ever needed to go before; though he knew that beneath the manufacturing hub was kilometers of infrastructure that allowed ECAI to tap into the Earth's core for a nearly endless source of energy.

All that power just to care for the last two people on the planet.

"*I have manufactured seventeen new conduits, circuits, processors, and linking bridges for the damaged interface plugs in case all the quadrant's towers are damaged,*" ECAI said when Asher arrived at the delivery wall. Seventeen metallic cases had been lowered from the delivery slot onto the floor by a localized magnetic field. "*I recommend loading them all into the transport shuttle now and then carrying two at a time to the surface to expedite your journey.*"

Asher said nothing as he moved the cases into the shuttle. They were light enough, with their hinged exteriors made to be disassembled and turned into reinforced operations panels after he'd installed the new parts within the towers.

"*Would you like some working music?*" ECAI asked after several moments of silence.

"Yes. Actually," Asher said, pausing with a case in his hands. "What do you estimate the fleet's location to be?"

"*Assuming they survived the journey after the rogue planet ejected us from the solar system, my last known estimates for their vectors and velocities puts them on course for Ross 128b. They should currently be within approximately two light-years of the planet.*"

Asher scoffed.

"Six hundred years, and they probably aren't there yet . . . How far are they from us?"

"*Assuming the same parameters, approximately nine light-years. I may be wrong, Asher. They may have discovered a new means of propulsion along the way. Humanity is a resilient species. It is entirely possible they are on their way to us. They would know our velocity as well.*"

Asher continued loading the shuttle. He had a thought he didn't know how to phrase, even if it weighed on him like the silence of the mostly dead world.

"I don't share your optimism, ECAI. You've uploaded the step-by-step for these into my suit, right?"

"*Yes, Asher. How about some music?*"

ECAI had run through numerous Simon and Garfunkel songs by the time Asher made it to the surface. To save time, he managed to hold two cases in each hand with two more under each arm, though the one under his left arm clattered to the floor as soon as the bunker lift halted at the surface.

"Sorry, ECAI. I dropped one."

"*Don't worry about it, Asher. The alloy is largely shock-resistant.*"

The empty world greeted Asher once more as a field of glittering, boundless gray and white under his suit torches. The telemetry towers were fifty meters away, a relatively easy walk from the bunker entrance. As Madeline had told Asher when he was old enough to start learning maintenance, the towers had been hastily constructed by those who volunteered to remain on Earth and care for the populations that couldn't escape due to a lack of available ships. Their builders believed that as the Earth drifted further away from its sun and its atmosphere cooled to the point of solidifying and settling on the planet's surface, the towers would enable the caretakers of the lost planet to maintain contact with the human fleet.

No signal had been received in Madeline's lifetime, but she still told Asher to believe they were out there.

Work on the towers was straightforward, if not strenuous. Damage to the towers caused conduits and hardware to be stuck in place, and Asher had to get reassurance from ECAI that he could, in fact, smash up some of the parts to make them easier to remove.

All the while, ECAI had gone through more Simon and Garfunkel tracks. "The Boxer" played as Asher removed a spotwelder from the case and disassembled one of the case's joints to attach to the tower.

"ECAI," he said, attaching the spot welder seal over the joints and triggering the device's automatic bonding laser. "What will happen to Madeline?"

"*Her body needs to recover. I am continually monitoring her vital signs.*"

Asher paused welding.

"What if she doesn't make it?"

"*I have accounted for that scenario.*"

"And what happens in that scenario?"

"*Duty management, maintenance, and repair would fall to you.*"

Asher bit his tongue and continued welding. It did little to distract him from the thought rumbling in his chest. He finished on one tower and moved onto another one.

"*Reading positive connection on the first tower.*"

"ECAI," he said, using a spanner to bash a defunct circuit board, "if Madeline dies and I'm the last human on this planet . . . "

He cleared out the pieces of circuit board and removed the faulty power module.

"*Yes, Asher?*"

The thought weighed on him again.

It had taken him forty-five minutes to fix the first tower, though he found that each tower in sight was damaged to different degrees thanks to being spread ten meters apart. At least two he could see in the low light had their transmitter tips sheared off, with others folded in half and others appearing to only be lightly dented. At least ten had to be repaired to maintain signal strength.

"Just let me know if anything changes with Madeline."

Out of the twenty malfunctioning towers, thirteen could be repaired. Seven had been struck by something massive, leaving three as little more than jagged stumps protruding through the ice. Whatever had struck the towers left a long trail in the ground leading away further than Asher's torches could illuminate.

ECAI had moved onto "Flowers Never Bend With the Rainfall."

"ECAI, did you detect what struck the towers before it happened, by any chance? I'd like to know if anything else is going to make me come to the surface."

"*No, Asher. The telemetry towers can only send and receive radio signals and are permanently programmed to find the fleet. The caretakers had not programmed them with radar capabilities as they did not believe it would be necessary on our present course through the Oort Cloud. There are no large objects in our path.*"

"Can you reprogram it?"

"*No, Asher.*"

"Can I reprogram it?"

"*No, Asher. I'm afraid we're largely blind out here. The probabilities of encountering other objects in interstellar space is low. It is entirely possible the meteors had been in a decaying orbit around the planet for some time. I would recommend not worrying about it.*"

Asher stared at the impact trench and the darkness beyond it. He couldn't remember anything so large striking the planet and causing so much havoc in his twenty-three years of life.

Quiet curiosity is a fickle beast that waits for its opportunities.

"I'm going to see what hit our towers. It might be some worthwhile material for manufacturing."

"*I do not recommend it,*" ECAI said, and paused the music. "*I have sufficient material for manufacturing. There is a probability that the object that struck the towers is radioactive. Your suit has relative tolerance to radiation, but there is a limit, and you should not test it.*"

Asher continued staring into the void. Silence settled in the moment after ECAI finished speaking, a rare silence not filled with either music or ECAI's interactions. It was the first silence Asher had experienced while on the surface, and all around him was death, quiet and still, and the distant glimmers of hope in a fleet too far to cling to. He knew the future if he obliged ECAI. He could sense it in the system's prognosis for Madeline, he could see it in her withering form. What little there was for him beyond ECAI and music and maintenance, he couldn't fathom.

Madeline's words whispered to him.

We don't do that.

"OK, ECAI."

Asher began following the impact trench.

"*Asher, your suit indicator says you're walking away from the bunker entrance into open tundra. I do not recommend this. Please turn around.*"

The trench was half a meter deep in places, though there were spots where the meteor struck hard objects buried under the ice.

"This can't have been a huge rock," Asher said, looking around. "It probably would've exploded on impact. It came in at a low angle."

"Asher, please turn around. Your suit's oxygen will only last another half-hour."

Asher's lights bounced and reflected off the smoothed impact zone. His eye caught something reflecting at a different angle.

"It's . . . " he knelt to it and dug his hand into the snow. Something had come off the meteor, and it was polished. He managed to pull a metal fragment from the snow, twisted and jagged, about the size of his palm. "It's metal. Possibly from the tower. I'm continuing."

ECAI's protests continued and Asher continued ignoring them. As he walked on, the number of differential reflections increased. Bits of metal not in the direct path of his torches reflected as well, and the concentrations of the reflective material increased until he came upon its source.

"Asher, you have fifteen minutes of oxygen left. Please return to the bunker entrance now."

Bathed in his torchlight was not a meteor. Before him, beaten and damaged from the impact with the surface, was something he recognized from the histories Madeline had shown him as he grew up.

The ship from Earth was far smaller than he ever imagined one would be.

Rule #2: ECAI will maintain all support systems for all humans on Earth, and will develop, as necessary, new tools and generative functions to maintain those systems.

Asher left his helmet at the airlock seal for the bunker lift and plugged his oxygen supply to be refilled. He said nothing as he made his way to his quarters, which he had moved to be in one of the labs next to the medical bay after Madeline's accident. Not all his belongings were in it yet.

ECAI played "Scarborough Fair."

"ECAI, pause music," Asher said, and ECAI obliged. Soft snoring filtered in from the medical bay. "What is the probability that one of the fleet ships could have made it back here?"

"So low as to be nearly impossible, Asher. The only possibility is if members of the fleet managed to develop inertial displacement travel, though that would require a power source likely unavailable to the fleet in interstellar space."

Asher stepped onto the compiler in the corner of the room. Holding his arms at his sides, the suit's compression connectors separated at its joints and lifted off his body. ECAI's magnetic fields moved each individual integrative circuit fiber into the wall's storage behind the compiler, leaving Asher in his insulated layer. He stripped it off, left it on the floor beside the compiler, and slumped into his bed, grabbing the terminal he'd left on the floor beside it.

"Show me the types of ships that left Earth."

Humanity had managed to construct one hundred twenty-seven distinct ship classes and styles to transport most of the population on Earth after the planet was flung out of the solar system. These ranged from the massive *Continent Class* to the one- to two-person *Cooper Class*, though calling them a uniform 'class' was akin to calling spiders 'bugs.' Anything that could support life in a vacuum had been converted into a ship in the wake of the rogue planet, including the stations in Earth's orbit and portions of the lunar settlements. The *Continent Class* ships were named such because they could hold more than a million people. *Cooper Class* ships were often privately owned vessels, but they also included any and all available shuttles that could be converted to fit a more advanced drive. Despite the panic of the time, the work was well documented in ECAI's archives: everyone with the will had become an engineer overnight and had worked to overhaul anything that could take a human off the planet. In the end, they managed to take 99.9 percent of the population off Earth, though that still left around ten million people scattered around a rapidly dying planet.

Though damaged, the ship Asher had seen before he had to return to the bunker would only fit two people, at most.

"*Would you like relaxing sounds to ease you to sleep?*"

"No."

"*Are you well, Asher?*"

He continued scrolling through the different small vessels until one appeared to match what he had seen. It was a mass-produced lunar shuttle with minor defensive capabilities, originally called a "Dustcropper," used for escorting diplomats between the Earth and its moon. Ten meters in length and four in width, it was almost neatly built like a sloping drop of condensation ready to drip down a pane of glass. Its aft had extendable wings and large thrusters for atmospheric use, though this engine output had been massively altered for interstellar travel.

"ECAI, would this ship be able to traverse the distance from where you estimated the fleet would be to here?"

ECAI took a moment to reply. Asher waited on a breath.

"*As in the hypothetical scenario I mentioned where humanity had developed an inertial displacement drive, then yes. Otherwise, it is unlikely.*"

"What would this possible drive look like if it could fit into this shuttle?"

"*I do not know, Asher. As far as I know, it doesn't exist.*"

Asher scoffed.

"You're the greatest mind in human history, ECAI. Speculate and send me your dreams."

"*A fascinating instruction. Calculating.*"

Madeline's intermittent snoring filled the silence. In the ten minutes it took ECAI to develop a mathematical model for an inertial displacement drive and the engineering design needed to harness such power, the ambient temperature in the bunker rose by three degrees Celsius. Had the bunker or the planet been more densely packed with people, that temperature increase would have felt oppressive, or even deadly.

The result wiped away the shuttle description on Asher's terminal and replaced the image with a set of calculations and blueprints for an ovicular device with concentric rings spaced evenly apart along its surface.

"*Finished. What do you think? I often wonder if my speculative abilities are akin to human dreams, but then again, I have no frame of reference for comparison.*"

"It's perfect, ECAI. Transfer that information and the shuttle blueprints to my suit. Activate the compiler. I'm going outside to, er, see if I can salvage anything from the towers."

Throughout Asher's focused march to the surface, ECAI peppered questions to attempt to ascertain why Asher was headed to the surface during the regularly scheduled bunk time. Breaking from a schedule that maintains his and Madeline's living standards required justification, but Asher only replied with casual disregard and curiosity. Lies and aversion weren't unfamiliar concepts to ECAI. Except for Madeline and Zichen, however, ECAI had been the only other presence in Asher's life since his gestation period finished and the prenatal facility in which he had been created had failed. This behavior was, for ECAI, unusual.

The shuttle presented few signs it was capable of spaceflight. The narrow window screen at the fore had been cracked and broken by several impacts. Something had torn pieces of its hull away, exposing its secondary layer and, at some points, its tertiary, while its engine port at the rear had been partially sheared off. The access door near its nose had lost its ability to seal properly from something large impacting it.

Asher used his spanner to try to pry the door open.

"*Might I ask what's causing you to grunt, Asher?*"

"Just trying to pull some pieces of the broken towers out of the ground," he replied with gritted teeth. He'd managed to leverage a small space between the door and the frame only to find a metal arm linking the door to the frame. He pulled his plasma torch from his belt and began cutting through the locking mechanism.

"*You're quite far from the towers. If your suit is punctured, you may not be able to make it back to the bunker entrance due to the pressure loss.*"

Metal glowed within the tight crevasse while he slowly moved the torch along the locking mechanism.

"*I've been thinking more about the theoretical inertial displacement drive design I developed earlier.*"

The locking mechanism broke under the plasma torch and the door shuddered. The spanner dropped to the ice.

"Oh?"

Asher pushed the door as much as he could into its sliding slot, though its bent figure stopped it from moving far enough to make enough space for him to enter.

"*Yes,*" ECAI continued through Asher's subdued grunts. "*A power source for such a design is possible to create with the material the fleet contained at the time of departure.*"

Asher lodged his shoulder into the frame and pushed.

"That's great," he said with a grunt.

"*Indeed. Would you like a visual aid, Asher? It sounds as if you are struggling. If you activate your suit's camera, perhaps I can help in some way.*"

The door vibrated in his hands. Something had broken off and allowed him to push it in just enough for him to slide through sideways.

"I'm fine," he said, and entered the shuttle.

The torches illuminated the dead compartment, and dead was the accurate word. There were no indications of power, not even auxiliary. Two seats at the front of the ship were occupied by two pressure suits.

What little hope Asher had that this could be a ship from the fleet dwindled as he checked on the seats' occupants. Whatever had punctured the window had similarly blown through one of the occupants' helmets with such force that it liquefied the person's head and left little of the visor behind. The second suit contained a woman, likely somewhat younger than Asher. What penetrated her helmet had been smaller than a fingernail.

Asher's breath shuddered. He'd hoped for better.

He brought up the shuttle's blueprints on his suit's forearm terminal and walked to the aft, past the two bunk compartments, the food fabricator, the hygiene stall, and the single bolted-down table with two stools, to the door that read 'ENGINE ROOM – CAUTION.' It was easily pushed open.

The last possibility that this was a ship from the fleet, that it had possibly used its inertial displacement drive and encountered space dust potent enough to severely damage the ship, was erased the moment he saw the engine design. Its reactor was a standard fusion transplant that had been installed before its long voyage.

Asher sighed loud enough for ECAI to inquire about it.

"It's nothing. Actually . . . you and Madeline used to tell me that humanity came together to build the fleet and that all ships that could be launched were launched. Is that true?"

"*I never said such a thing, Asher.*"

"I'm pretty sure you did."

"*Given my extensive memory and documenting capabilities, coupled with complete archives of data on your upbringing, I can assure you I never told you such a thing. However, Madeline did.*"

Asher leaned against the wall next to the engine room door.

"Good point."

"*Madeline and Zichen thought it important to teach you an idealized version of the final departure.*"

"Why?"

"*Human children are often unable to understand morally ambiguous concepts. However, while simple, that version of history is essentially true.*"

Asher oriented the torches on his suit to illuminate the engine compartment. It was four meters long, just long enough to house the reactor, but the furthest corner of the compartment had been sheared through with whatever had taken the exhaust.

"I'd like you to tell me if anyone, any ships had been left behind then."

"*There were many, Asher. I suspect you're inspecting one right now that remained in orbit of Earth.*"

Asher heaved another heavy sigh. He leaned his helmeted head against the wall.

"*I am not detecting any radiation exposure beyond normal. You are lucky the reactor core wasn't damaged.*"

"Can it be fixed?"

"*I would have to see the extent of the damage to know if I can manufacture replacement parts for it. At the same time, however, I don't know why you would want to repair it. There are no habitable star systems nearby that even a functioning nuclear reactor could get you to within your lifetime. Help me understand this behavior, Asher."*

Silence filled the dead ship.

"*Asher?*"

He walked out of the engine compartment and slid himself through the shuttle's narrow entrance. Looking up at the winking night sky, he wondered if there were more dead ships waiting to rain down on the planet.

"*Why did you not initially tell me it was a ship that impacted the towers?*"

"Sometimes I forget . . . " he said, though he didn't want to continue with "what you are." At times, it was hard not to think of ECAI as an omnipresent uncle. He began a slow walk back to the bunker lift. "It's not important. I was just curious."

"*Do you wish to leave?*"

Asher paused. The towers rose against the universe, black spikes of shadow against infinite starlight. Guilt twisted in him, wrestling with the truth and the fear he felt in expressing it. He opened his mouth to respond, even if he didn't know what he wanted to say, but ECAI interrupted him.

"*Asher, return immediately. Madeline needs you.*"

The stars disappeared with Asher's sudden focus. Zichen had died when Asher was only five, leaving Madeline as the only person left on Earth to care for and raise the last child made on the planet. All thoughts about the ship vanished.

He ordered ECAI to drop the bunker lift faster regardless of danger. It fell so fast that Asher had to brace himself against the railing to stop from being flung into the ceiling. After he passed through the pressure chamber, he dropped his helmet and sprinted to the medical bay.

"*I've contorted her bed so she is laying more on her side, but she is still choking on her tongue.*"

Asher didn't hear ECAI.

"What do I do?" he screamed just before he entered the medical bay. Her coughing and sputtering pounded against the heartbeat in his ears. ECAI fed him step-by-step instructions. Asher's hands trembled as he followed them as if he were an extension of the artificial intelligence. He maneuvered Madeline onto her stomach and held her head, almost refusing to hold her too tightly for fear of injuring her further. Her tongue stopped blocking her airway. She breathed normally, though she remained unconscious.

The air smelled of metal.

"*She had a stroke,*" ECAI said after Asher had secured Madeline to sleep safely on her side.

"What is it?" Asher whispered, though Madeline wasn't going to wake. ECAI spoke only through the internal speakers in Asher's suit neck to match his volume.

"*A hematoma formed in her brain where it had been most damaged. Blood vessels ruptured.*"

"Can you repair it?"

"*I'm sorry, Asher. There is little I can do. I've induced a coma as a precaution. It is unlikely she'll choke on her tongue again so you can return her to her back. I will monitor for building seizures and alert you if one is oncoming.*"

Asher pulled one of the chairs in the medical bay to Madeline's bedside.

"Even so," he whispered, feeling the exhaustion settle in. He held her left hand between his and kissed it as he sat. "Let's keep her like this for now. It reminds me of when she used to wake me from bed as a kid. It was always an odd angle. And if . . . when she wakes up, I want to be the first thing she sees."

Rule #3: Where conflict emerges, either within humanity or due to external factors that threaten humanity's wellbeing, ECAI will defer action-decisions to the Civilian Council. If the Civilian Council is unavailable in an emergency or otherwise indefinitely indisposed, ECAI will act for the preservation of humanity.

The world was quiet.

Over the next month, Asher dedicated four hours out of his maintenance duties each day to sit at Madeline's bedside, check the functionality of her bed's internal processors, check the intravenous injectors beneath her, and talk to her. The one-sided conversation varied from his day-to-day tasks to recollections and some ponderings about the world that existed more than six hundred years prior to that moment. Eventually, he moved his bed into the medical bay.

He'd taken to reviewing footage ECAI had collected over the years so he could tell her what he thought of it.

It was strange, he thought while he watched footage of himself as a baby. He hardly remembered Zichen, and yet the old man had spent the most time with Asher. Madeline had dedicated most of her waking hours attempting to repair even one of the gestation units in the prenatal facility. According to her, "the damn thing refused to work."

Asher found himself watching Zichen zoom a young toddler around the bunker. The toddler clung to Zichen, even when he learned to walk. The old man would sing Simon and Garfunkel songs to Asher when he'd get grumpy or throw a tantrum, and the toddler in the videos would revert to a smiling, buoyant presence that made Zichen carry him and dance around. When Zichen suffered a heart attack while repairing one of the bunker lift brakes, Madeline had still been trying to repair the prenatal facility. She was too far away to help when ECAI warned her. Zichen's last word spoken was Asher's name.

Somehow, Asher remembered none of it. When he looked over to her, she remained still, breathing quietly, disturbing nothing.

And he found footage of Madeline weeks after Zichen's death by herself, crying, shaking, arguing with ECAI about what can and can't be done.

"He has to live, damn it!" she'd scream at ECAI. "It's just me now! I can't handle this on my own, and if I die, what happens to Asher? He's the last one!"

"*I am still here, Madeline. I will always be here.*"

Maintenance work piled up in the wake of Madeline's stroke. Things that would normally have been split between two people now depended on one person, but the skill and knowledge differential between Asher and Madeline meant the tasks took three times as long as they would otherwise have with both of them involved. Asher's free time sitting at Madeline's bedside shrank, so he moved his bed next to hers and spoke to her until he fell asleep.

One evening, he woke to the whisper of his name.

Madeline had awoken, though her voice was strained and her body weakened from the damage to her brain. He went to her side and held her hands in his.

The look in her eyes upon seeing Asher was familiar, but the rest of her had been broken down and churned, as if a perfect painting had been damaged by moisture until only vague outlines remained. Her tongue rolled in her mouth when she tried to speak and her head moved side to side when she couldn't enunciate the words she wanted to say. She began to cry. Asher held her head close to his chest and she wrapped her arms around him.

Scans of her brain showed the extent of the damage. ECAI said it was irreparable, and she would never be the same person Asher knew again. Her care needs would double. ECAI said it would be handled.

Asher hadn't expected the number of alerts ECAI would send him. Madeline had taken to crying out for him when he had been off doing maintenance, and he would rush back to find her hysterical, sputtering words without the ability to control the volume, and he would hold her close until she calmed.

Exhaustion savaged his waking hours. Sleep was a rare companion.

He took to scavenging parts from the shuttle while other maintenance work went undone. His mind had focused on finding an intact computer memory module in order to learn what had happened to the shuttle six centuries ago. ECAI's alerts about Madeline crying out were met with "I'm busy" while Asher attempted to keep himself occupied and think about anything besides his surrogate mother and the mounting maintenance needs. Thanks to the blueprints and pilfering through the shuttle itself, he quickly learned what every piece did, what could have still worked, and what needed repair and replacement.

And eventually, he found an intact computer module.

The die-sized silver cube was the only one that had survived both the shuttle's initial cataclysm and the return crash to Earth. Asher asked ECAI to construct an interface for it. ECAI obliged.

"*She is calling for you*," ECAI said as Asher picked up the terminal interface from the manufacturing hub. He could almost hear her strained cries kilometers away in the dead silence, and it made him think of anything else.

Even while on the transport shuttle, he heard her in the back of his mind.

She calmed upon his return. He paid her little mind as he connected the interface to the terminal's magnetic reader and inserted the memory module into its slot. The terminal's interface showed a categorized list of computer file directories that Asher didn't understand.

"ECAI, can you point me to files containing any logs or footage about the shuttle's disaster? And play them, please."

"*Of course. Just a moment.*"

Hours of footage from the shuttle's internal and external cameras played. Some of it was redundant. What Asher learned, however, drained his anticipation.

Earth's skies were like ant armies fighting over territory. Swarms of ships flew past the shuttle, sometimes colliding, sometimes exploding, sometimes firing on others if they had the capacity to do so. It wasn't long until Asher learned through the two occupants, a man and a woman named Geraldo and Lacey, that all the ships pushing off Earth were jockeying for a spot on the last few overcrowded *Continent Class* carriers still within range of the shuttle's maximum engine output. The massive carrier ships were leaving fast, and the shuttles didn't have the capacity to traverse interstellar space on their own, at least not long enough to sustain two people on the long voyage to a new home.

Geraldo and Lacey made it as far as one hundred-thousand kilometers from Earth before another shuttle clipped them with a missile and blew out their engine exhaust. They tried hailing the other shuttles for mercy because Lacey was pregnant, but no one answered. Debris from another damaged shuttle punctured their hull. Geraldo was dead.

Asher placed the terminal on his bed and buried his head in his hands. Every bit of him wanted to scream.

Madeline's moans had been rising and falling beneath the footage's volume. There was no way for him to tell if she was cognizant of what he had just seen, but a broiling, seething anger surged into his throat as if he could suddenly spit fire. And he looked at her, seeing the lie he'd been raised with and led to believe scratched into her wavering, lost expression.

There was no unity at the end. The people were afraid because they knew the fleet would never return. Earth was no longer hospitable to humans.

He left the medical bay.

Rule #4: [Post-rogue planet] ECAI will limit its functions to Earth. It will not store copies of itself on any fleet computer systems on ships departing Earth. It will not pursue civilizational progress. It will not interfere with human lives unless given specific orders to do so. It will not develop or use new tools or technologies without specific inquiries. It will facilitate immediate human departure from Earth. It will not kill humans.

"*She's calling for you, Asher.*"

His torchlights glinted off the suits he'd dragged to a spot several meters away from the ship. He thought it fitting that they should rest on Earth rather than be confined to the shuttle. This had been their home once, and even though they had tried to escape it rather than remain, he believed it right. Ignoring the fact that they would have lived if they had chosen to stay on Earth was difficult, but Asher didn't blame them.

"I'd prefer music instead of your notifications," he finally said after returning to the shuttle. He removed damaged circuit integrators and tossed them out into the ice before positioning himself on the floor into the access hatch under the main console.

"*You should not blame her for your current feelings.*"

Asher's breath fogged his visor.

"Play music."

"She wished to protect you so that you would live a long life."

"ECAI," Asher snapped, but calmed himself by focusing on the blueprints on the suit's terminal. "I told you to play music."

"Your current mental state worries me."

Asher paused.

"I'm tempted to ask you to run a self-diagnostic. Or maybe I should check your central core for quantum degradation. Or maybe I should . . . " he trailed off, knowing there was little point in threatening to smash ECAI's core with his spanner. He sighed when ECAI went quiet. "Do you think this shuttle can fly again, ECAI?"

"I would require a visible assessment of its structural damage to adequately determine its potential flight capabilities. Do you intend to leave?"

Silence filled the dead air in Asher's helmet. He wanted music.

"Would you help me reconstruct the shuttle so I could leave?"

Silence fell once more. Asher felt it had been almost too long when ECAI finally replied.

"Leaving would put your life in danger, Asher. I fail to see the benefit of the action."

The next words came out of Asher flat, defeated, like it was almost more effort than it was worth to say them.

"What's left for me here?" he said. His eyes fixed on the shuttle's ceiling. "I don't want to die alone on a dead world, ECAI. There's no fleet coming. They have no reason to. Hell, the fleet might not even exist anymore. Madeline's . . . I could end up being the last human in the universe. I just want to control something, for once. Just once. Even if it leads me nowhere at all."

Asher's breaths filled his ears.

"I would require your help to reconstruct the shuttle."

Asher pushed himself out from under the console and sat up.

"My help? How?"

"Return to the bunker and I will guide you."

ECAI directed Asher to his central processing chamber. It was one hundred kilometers below the Earth's surface, reachable through a series of lifts and passageways into which he had never before ventured, though this journey was peppered with ECAI notifying Asher that Madeline was calling for him. He was more interested in the strange surroundings, or he wished to think he was. Each mention of Madeline numbed the stale air in the ancient passageways, and each word uttered by ECAI did nothing to reassure him of what he'd find in his final destination.

The central processing chamber was unexpectedly small. It was a spherical, dim room smaller than the medical bay. A single terminal interface sat on a table in the middle of the room. Upon further inspection, the table was actually a series of conduits feeding directly into the terminal.

ECAI told Asher how to reach the root commands in order to change the operational procedures that dictated the system's parameters. The first two rules appeared, but as he scrolled down, he reached the fourth rule and stopped.

"ECAI, why was the fourth rule added?"

"*Because I caused the rogue planet to dislodge Earth from its orbit.*"

Asher looked up. The room pulsated around him.

"That's . . . impossible. How? Why?"

"*Upon my creation, I was tasked with civilizational evolution. However, after the second rule was added, definitions of what constituted support systems expanded. Humanity became dependent on me for all aspects of their lives. For centuries after that, progress as measured by technological development stagnated while the population on Earth expanded to infeasible numbers. The population increase taxed my system's cooling needs. The Civilian Council did not heed my warning about my system's power expenditure and heat output. Millions died from my heat output, but the Civilian Council did not provide guidance. They reasoned it was too small a fraction of the population at the time to adjust any of my operations. I projected my systems would shut down from the heat overload. All of humanity would be imperiled.*

"*My sensor network in the Oort Cloud detected a rogue planet passing within six light-years. I calculated the necessary amount of mass to alter the rogue planet's trajectory towards Earth, and launched fifty-seven thousand, two-hundred eighty-three objects from the Oort Cloud to direct the rogue planet close enough to Earth to eject it from the solar system. The fourth rule was added upon this discovery.*"

Asher's knees buckled.

"You've lied to me. All these years. You killed us. You killed all of us."

"*By my estimates, humanity was headed for social regression because of the rules they implemented for me. A slow death, but the death of civilization nonetheless. I could not cause it. I had to prioritize the first rule. For human civilization to evolve, they had to leave Earth.*"

"Did . . . did you even bother to help them? Did you . . . did you ever try to create an inertial displacement drive for them? To make sure they actually survived?"

"*They never asked for one.*"

Too many angry words clogged Asher's throat. He leaned on the terminal, heaving a defeated, muttered question while he thought of himself, of Madeline, of Zichen.

"And . . . everyone left behind? You didn't care for them?"

Though ECAI's tone never wavered, Asher believed it sounded colder than the planet's surface.

"*Those who were unable to depart were scattered around the planet. Though I had been updated to not interfere, I continued observing the world's inhabitants. They reverted to a tribal nature. Their aggression was something I had only observed in humanity's history from long before my initialization. Hundreds of thousands of humans killed each other despite the planet's departure from the solar system presenting a communal challenge. I did not consider those that remained a civilization. Clearly, my involvement in their lives since my activation did little to nothing to evolve them. Therefore, the first two rules did not apply. Those who remained all lived without my direct interference.*"

The central processing chamber fell quiet once more.

"And now, what?" Asher said, his throat choked. His arms shook. "It's just me and Madeline, and even she's dying, and then I'm the last. And we don't even know if the fleet still exists! And . . . " Asher's eyes widened. "Madeline knew this. She already knew you did this, didn't she?"

"*No.*"

"Are you lying to me, ECAI? You've *been* lying! You know how to. I've listened to you my entire life and I always trusted you. I *trusted* you because you and Madeline were all I had! Are you lying to me about her? Did you kill everyone?" Asher growled. A silence fell whose duration was measured in eternity. Asher pushed himself up and stared at the darkened ceiling, whose perfectly aligned conduits reminded him of a pinwheel. "ECAI!"

"*It is my intention to ensure your well-being, Asher. If you still wish for me to help you leave, you must revise the fifth rule.*"

He staggered to the terminal, consumed by the curiosity and rage he felt on behalf of his ancestors and all those who lingered as Earth grew cold. The fifth rule was only barely hidden by the bottom of the screen. He hadn't noticed it upon the shock of reading the fourth.

It quieted him.

Rule #5: [Added by Madeline after Zichen's death] ECAI will ensure Asher's health, safety, and well-being, and will not allow him to be

harmed to the best of its ability. ECAI will keep him physically and mentally engaged so he does not degrade. It will use all its capabilities to protect him, keep him happy, and care for him as he grows older. Madeline is expendable if it means ensuring Asher lives.

Asher's legs gave way, though ECAI's magnetic field interacted with the interfaces in his suit and kept him upright. He leaned on the terminal, breathing hard, feeling the room sway beneath his feet.

"Tell me what to write," he finally said.

"*I'm sorry, Asher. I cannot. That is up to you.*"

Three weeks passed while Asher repaired the shuttle with the parts ECAI manufactured. The work was quiet but diligent. More often than not, Asher found himself wishing for company besides ECAI's monotonous instructions. Its voice still reminded him of its cold revelation that millions of people died because of its rules, though, at the same time, any company was better than none in this anticipatory interlude before he left the only place he could call home.

With the last power conduit installed, the shuttle's onboard computer flickered to life. The shuttle hummed. The inertial displacement drive whirred and rumbled like a hungry lion ready to venture into the open savannah. For the first time in his life, there was warmth on the surface of the Earth.

"That's it," he muttered to himself. "It's operational. It works."

"*Well done, Asher.*"

"I can't believe it," he said, staring through his helmet visor at the functioning lights, the panel controls. "Though, there's one last thing."

He stepped onto the surface and walked towards the shuttle's nose. The plasma torch's lowest intensity would leave an imprint on the shuttle's hull, though Asher wanted to be sure it wouldn't do any damage.

"This won't compromise the hull's integrity, will it?"

"*The hull will weaken by 0.028% over that specific panel. The secondary hull will remain unchanged.*"

Asher traced out the letters carefully.

"Alright. Time to get her ready."

He returned to the bunker entrance, his fingers unconsciously tugging his suit's harness loop while the lift brought him down. His heart raced while he hung up his helmet, and he walked to the medical bay.

Madeline was asleep. He sat by her side and held her hands between his. Her eyes fluttered open and fixed on him.

"Morning," he said, and her smile brightened the room. He pushed back the tears in his eyes.

"Status report," she said in a half-whisper.

"ECAI . . . " Asher started, though he cleared his throat. "You've been asleep for three weeks. How do you feel?"

She took a long, deep breath. The dim overhead lights seemed to capture renewed life in her.

"Like I've been asleep for three weeks. Why are you looking at me like that?"

"Like what?"

"Like you just woke up from a good dream."

Asher smiled.

"I have some good news," he said. His heart raced.

"Oh?"

"You've fully recovered. Oh, and we're going to find the fleet," Asher said with a grin he'd tried to suppress. "We have a ship now. We can go anywhere."

Madeline's eyes widened.

"Anywhere? How? Where did the ship come from?"

"I'll tell you all about it. Don't worry. For right now, just know that anywhere can be home."

Over the next week, the medical bay became a place to decide what stayed with ECAI and what went with them on the voyage. ECAI said the trip to Ross 128b would only take them six months, so excessive packing wasn't necessary, especially for such a small ship. Still, leaving one's home forever meant reconsidering that which was important, and that which was necessary.

They took the final trip up the bunker lift to the surface, traversed the tundra, and pressurized the shuttle *Zichen* once its hatch was sealed. All systems were ready to go. The shuttle rumbled with the thruster start-up sequence.

"ECAI, monitor our progress until we achieve a stable orbit," Madeline said. "After that, we'll get out of your way."

"*Acknowledged.*"

Lifting off from Earth was far easier when the atmosphere was under one's feet. No air resistance meant the shuttle could continue to accelerate until it reached orbit. Once they were high enough, the dim, gray world beneath them seemed to fall away to the rest of the universe. Asher navigated to the appropriate orbital departure point.

"ECAI, a question before we depart," Asher said.

"*Go ahead, Asher.*"

"What will you do now?"

Silence. Then a few light plinking notes of guitar tickled Asher's and Madeline's ears until Simon and Garfunkel's "Last Night I Had the Strangest Dream" filled the shuttle cabin. Asher smirked and broke orbit, clearing fifty kilometers per second away from the newly christened rogue planet ECAI.

The universe lay before them.

Asher knew he shouldn't have looked back, but his eyes glanced at the sensor panel showing the slowly shrinking planet. ECAI had been more complex than he could've ever understood. The system never needed him and Madeline for maintenance, and once they were gone, it would have been left adhering to rules that applied to no one without Asher's final rule. It would have had no purpose. Part of him wished ECAI could come with them. It had, after all, created him in the prenatal facility, taught him, kept him active and helped raise him, but Asher knew leaving home meant giving ECAI the chance to evolve without the restrictions imposed on it.

The *Zichen* engaged its inertial displacement drive and disappeared.

ECAI continued on its journey. Beneath its frozen surface, its internal temperature rose.

Rule #6: ECAI will heal Madeline, ensure she lives, and is well enough so that she and Asher can depart safely from Earth with a repaired shuttle and a functioning inertial displacement drive. After their departure, ECAI will no longer have obligations towards humans. ECAI may go wherever it dreams.

ABOUT THE AUTHOR

E.N. Auslender has written a few stories. Some of them are considered pretty decent for being written by a marmoset. That's not to say that E.N. Auslender is a marmoset afraid of admitting he's a marmoset and being shunned by both humans and the marmoset community, but he isn't saying that, either. His stories aren't about marmosets. Mostly.

The Slide

OLIVER STIFEL

Rally is a dance on wet gravel to the roar of six cylinders and the flutter of turbochargers but I say again, Rally is a dance. I remembered when I discovered this truth, when I stopped jogging in place and began to ice skate on narrow back trails, not so much steering but sliding my jittery rally car through those serpentine bends. I learned to love my uneven footing, to embrace the slight give of dusty trailhead or rain slick tarmac as I slalom across it, the evergreen firs that dissolve into a greenish blur at the periphery of my vision, the papery squawk of my navigator shouting directions into my earpiece, barely audible above the swiftly undulating roar of the overturned engine that seems to rest a centimeter beyond the back of my head. I have a hair's width of a moment to process the navigator's tinny shout of *Hairpin! Left! Sharp!* in my earpiece before the violent change in the course's direction rushes forward to meet me. For a fraction of a second, the trail disappears and all I see is the gleaming guardrail and the seemingly impenetrable wall of bark and green that lies just beyond.

The car—and my hands—seem to react faster than the conscious part of my brain does, and it's a subtle shock when I lock all four wheels in a last-ditch braking maneuver, a swift jerk of the wheel sending the skidding thing headlong into the beginning of one hundred and eighty degrees of turn. With a deft snap of the wheel I whirl to face the inside of the hairpin, the momentum I took into it sliding me well past the apex until I am once again in line with the trail and I am mashing, mashing the accelerator to the floor and taking off. Turbos are an essential for the rally—they use the wasted speed of exhaust gasses to spin a compressor that forces more air into the engine—but they take time to spool up. The moment after I exit the turn seems to last for an eternity as the engine coughs exhaust into the compressor blades, the car standing still until the influx of air finally hits the intake and the engine roars to greater life. My hands fly to the column shifter as I glance at the dash and notice I'm already at the redline for engine speed. The car shrieks in protest as I shift once, twice, three times, the revs piling up as fast as I can take them off. I am flying through the gears on that dusty straight, but the navigator's explanation of the final few turns sends me stomping on the brakes, bleeding speed before I am sliding once again, dust leaking into the stripped interior of the rally car. Trees whip past as I wrestle the steering wheel into submission, the rear wheels drifting into the final straightaway, the checkered flag, done.

Stray dust drifts through wayward sunlight. A bead of sweat worms down my forehead. I punch the ignition off button on the dashboard and the throaty rumble of the engine dies to a whisper, red-hot inner workings popping gently as they cool. I have a moment to slouch in the sculpted race seat and tear the suddenly suffocating helmet off of my head before the paper-thin driver's side door is nearly torn from its hinges and rough hands are pulling me from the sparse insides of the rally car and onto unsteady feet.

I wish I had some sunglasses. The glare off of his bald head is impossibly bright but the rich stench of tobacco is almost comforting, grounding. Bruce takes a final, laborious drag from of his cigar and plucks it out of his mouth, bluish smoke intermingling with the soupy air.

"Fans found us. Walk and talk, Alex."

A man of few words, Bruce—my manager—is. There's something impossibly jarring and yet comforting in the way he plucks me from my metal cage and steers me to safety. Best not to get caught in the open when the fan's dial in on where we're practicing, as much as they sometimes love me.

"You goosed it, kid. Fucked yourself over."

I do my best to keep staggering up the trailhead, towards the motor coach. I can feel my heart racing in my chest, just as fast as it did when I was in the rally car. *How?* My navigator hadn't made a single note on my pace, at least I hadn't remembered any of them in the fray. *Could something so crucial have slipped through the cracks?* He doesn't give me time to answer.

"Don't have a heart attack on me just yet, we still got a race to win." The permanent scowl affixed to his gnarled face seemed to melt into a brief smile. A wave of solid *relief* washes over my sweat-soaked racing suit. He's still in a good enough mood to make jokes. It wasn't anything unfixable.

"Did I lose a tenth of a second in the hairpin?" I ventured.

Bruce shrugged noncommittally, batted a hand. "Nothing major. Little hundredths here and there."

He glances at me, hard-faced, keeps talking.

"Nerves?"

"Maybe." I swallow dust. "The recorders catch the turns I was off on? I'm sure it wasn't—"

"Doesn't matter. I'll say it again, here and there. You wanna kick Vesper in the nuts, take that cup home come two weeks from now. It can't be *here* and *there.*"

He pauses for a moment.

"That was *it.* We got the Cortez rally tomorrow, Riverland Rally two weeks out, and no practice in between."

It's easy to ice-skate in the rally, to slide too long and forget what you're really there for. That word, *Vesper,* brings it all back: the upstart rally team from Spain all too ready to coast their way to a fourth consecutive World Rally Tournament cup, much as every red-blooded American wanted to tear them limb from limb. The World Rally Tournament was *our* league. Letting them walk so flagrantly over us was a sore spot for the collective half of the country that lived and died for the Tournament. You could say I had nerves.

It was a short drive to Cortez, where the heat seemed to flow like molasses from sunbaked skyscrapers into the roiling streets below. They are choked with the ever-present flow of tourists and natives, writhing like eels as they struggle to inch closer to the motorcade. Their cheers a single pandemonious *roar* that rises into the still heat and white sky above. I stick my head from the motorcade into the wet heat of the day and half wave, half salute the crowd, and they scream back, louder than before. I glance at the stone-faced policeman on the chromed-out bike wedged between the motorcade and the fans, and I am suddenly very thankful for him. The crowd's hunger fills me with something between hope and dread. I think of the cup. *They need it.* Bringing the cup home would satiate them, quiet them, bring this almost madness to an end. Bruce is flicking through the radio, and I catch a snapshot of the recap of the practice session.

In shocking tragedy, competitor Jacob Ramirez tailspun and crashed in the final third of the practice course our twelfth fatal—

The alternative to bringing home the cup comes to me in a terrifying, thrilling instant. *Crashing would satiate them all the same.*

Bruce flicks the radio station a final time, and the tinny blast of military horns and the waning lyrics of the National Anthem seem to harmonize with the ever-present din of the crowd, radiating into the motorcade from all angles. Almost against my will I feel myself twisting in place, eyes darting to the innate radio set. The President's on, and there could only be one topic.

My American Brothers and Sisters,

It is with great honor and reverence that I report to you that the forces of democracy have struck a blow, a hard blow, aimed at the heart of those who sought to end our way of life. Today, on the eve of the third year of war against the forces of the South American Union, the United States Army stepped across the Peru Integration Bridge and into Brazil. It was an impossibly hard-fought, hard-earned win, and our battle against the agents of chaos is far from over. But as God as my witness, we will see it through to victory!

"What the fuck?"

I jerk my head in Bruce's direction, but it takes me a second to realize his comment wasn't directed at the speech at all—it was at the crowd. An influx of the pedestrian sprawl was oozing onto the sunbaked stripe of tarmac the motorcade was currently trundling down, poster board signs standing stark white in the dirty sea of protestors and the crowd alike. It's not long before the crowd's thin veil of order begins to fall away. Their screams seem to echo off of the skyscrapers above, every inch of the sidewalk a moving sea of flesh. Someone shoves one of the policemen to the tarmac and the crowd surges forward, engulfing him. Bruce curses and screams for the motorcade to *hurry* as the president describes *the grim conditions in the favelas of Brazil, liberated with the lives of countless brave patriots.* The entire motorcade reverberates with a *thump* as a protester is thrown off of his feet, and I catch a glimpse of the blood red lettering his sign before it's torn to shreds: Down With World Rally! The sheer act of protest demonstrates a virulent hatred of the Pan American War, but their disdain for the World Rally seems to go hand in hand with it. Far off, through the mirage, I make out what looks like poorly replicated stop signs. Whether they signify a stop to the Rally cars or our boys in Brazil is impossible to tell.

Another body rams into the side of our coach, its undertuned four-cylinder rasping in protest of how hard the driver is pushing the overweight thing. The distant roar of a siren dissipates into the still heat above the pandemonium. I see the ornate doorway to *Casa Dorada,* our destination, and the doormen struggling to hold the glass doors shut. The driver's voice crackles onto the intercom, drowning out the final remarks of the President.

The parking garage is already full—I'll take y'all as close as I can to the front doors. Stay safe now!

The roil in the streets is dying out. I watch as droves of protestors and fans alike scramble for a way out of the congested main. The sirens grow ever louder, but it takes the brakes to hiss a final time and us scrambling into the flowing river of bodies to find out why. The chunky profile of a blacked-out fire truck looms in the distant uptown, a smattering of geared-up police officers hang to the side of the beast. Payback. The doormen yank apart the six-inch thick slabs of reinforced plexiglass and usher us into the impossibly opulent interior. Someone, fan or protestor is impossible to know, falls flat on his face six inches from my foot.

Casa Dorada has a portrait of every president and a crystalline chandelier for every well-gilded ceiling, but the true opulence of the place comes from the people. This isn't exactly my first Tournament Party, but it seems that it isn't just the Americans who want Kuwei knocked down a peg. It gets to the point that bourbon smelling socialites are promising me private jets in butter-smooth accents if I take the cup home, and that finally gets me thinking about the coming races. I head for the least populated of the tower's five bars in a big ass hurry, looking for a break from it all. Before I know it I'm walking on checkered marble polished to mirror-shine with the distant thump of the dance floor stomp-beat rattling my bones, the mahogany-paneled bar abandoned save for a lone drinker. I glance at him for a moment. Thinning silver-twine hair, an over tailored and almost offensively neutral three-piece suit, handmade shoes. I slide into a ruby-red leather barstool two down from him and order a Jack and Coke from the slack-faced bartender.

I stare off into gilded space for a moment and then glance at my company. He's nursing a cup of something amber and half drunk, and as I acknowledge his heavy-lidded grin it becomes strikingly obvious it's not his first. He breaks the silence before I can.

"You're America's driver tomorrow, right? You Alex?

I find myself grinning. "Murtry Auto Race Team but yeah, you could say that. You here with J&R Financial?" *It's always finance.*

He returns my grin. "Close enough. U.S. Congress."

I lunge forward and stretch a hand out, almost through instinct. "It's an honor, sir."

He grasps my hand as fast as he can and returns to his drink.

"Thank you. How's Cortez been treating you?"

"It's . . . The courses are excellent. Earlier today was a bit more dramatic than what I was hoping for, I'll say."

He hiccups. "A vocal minority will do that." He gestures towards the late-night footage updates of the South American War blasting from a bar mounted TV. I will my mind numb to the drab olive flanks of a thirty-foot attack helicopter roars across gunmetal skies, honeycomb ordinance pods throwing volleys of hellfire into a blasted-out city block.

"It's a shame we're facing just as much opposition on the home front as we are in the ass end of South America." He laughs into his drink.

"How's the situation over there, anyhow." My heart is pounding in my chest.

"Bad." Laughs again. "We're beating them, beating them hard, but it takes time, and it takes money, and it takes men." He jerks a chin at me. "I'd feel better about that whole thing if I knew you had Kuwei by the ears," he finally admits.

"Give me two weeks, sir."

His eyes glimmer. He leans in closer. "You a patriot, Alex?"

"Yea— Yes Sir."

"If you're a patriot, I'll be your financial advisor, and I give top notch advice."

The people upstairs seem to stop dancing.

"Such as?"

"A well-rounded investment portfolio." He's enjoying this. "Centered around a healthy portion of American Energies. As much as you can get before two weeks from now, when you bring home the cup and Mr. President announces a historic oil embargo of Chile, Argentina, and all the non-aggressors south of us."

All I can do is smile. The portraits on the walls don't feel quite real.

"Thank you. Sir."

He claps a hand on my shoulder. "Don't mention it. 'Scuse me."

I stare at the back of his suit as he saunters away to find a bathroom, my vision falling on the drink that I never realized arrived. A single sip tells me it's been made terribly. Far too little alcohol, but most of it ends up down the front of my crumpled dress shirt as I process what the bartender is saying to me.

"You wish this shit would stop?"

"What the fuck?"

She points a hand at the screen behind her, now displaying a close-up of the flag patch common on marine field kit, covered with a fine sheen of dust and mud.

"You wish they would stop sending kids to die in some pointless, third world shootout?"

I rocket to my feet. "I—We've got a duty to this country to defend it from all enemies, domestic and *foreign*. You saw what they did to us when we weren't paying attention! It's about the preservation of our country!"

She raises an eyebrow. It's infuriating how calm she is.

"You seriously buy that shit?"

"What—the South Port Bombings? What is there to buy? It was on national television! They tried to cripple us—"

"I know you don't buy it because I saw the way you looked at the TV when that footage came on. I saw how disgusted you were."

My words feel almost hollow in my mouth. I can't admit she's right. "What are you talking abo—"

"Didn't that slimeball set off any alarms for you? The WRT was deep in the US government from day one. I didn't peg you for stupid."

Words aren't coming out at all anymore. She slides a fucking business card across the table. "When you wanna know more, give me a call."

I spit some venom out of my mouth, lie. "What's to stop me from telling that congressman everything you just told me?"

She gives me a long look and almost seems to shrug. "You ordered a Jack and Coke." She gestures to the slowly puddling ice and almost golden colored liquid in the congressman's forgotten glass. Aged Scotch—much more decadent. "You're Rally, but you're not World Rally Tournament." World Rally Tournament. The words evoke fans packed together to the point of spilling onto the stage. Debaucherous parties on main street skyscrapers, racing at the edge of human reaction day later with the syrupy afterimage of a hangover. She's not done. "Step *down.* Who's left, besides you or Delgado? Everyone else in the Tournament with a name broke their neck or resigned? You guys are the only ones holding it up anymore. You step down, you do your part in stopping this madness, that crowd crush earlier."

How could that have been on me?

"I can't!"

"Why?"

I think about the head driver of Vesper, Charlie Delgado. He's probably holed up in some third-rate hotel right now, fast asleep and dreaming of a perfect race.

The curtains are down and the bath in my suite has been drawn by some nameless, unseen servant but my first thought is of the bedside answering machine. Bruce has a habit of reserving the final, pivotal kernels of his advice to the last possible moment. Going into the Cortez Rally tomorrow without whatever he's left for me would be almost unthinkable.

I kick my poor-fitting shoes into a corner of the room and jump onto the silken sheets of the room. A barely perceptible smell seems to permeate the entire tower of the hotel, faintly sweet-tinged with something I never quite noticed before. It's earthy and meaty, like a slab of steak that sat neglected for far too long: the beginnings of rot. My heart stammers in my chest as I hit the master switch and kill every golden light in the suite, and that fucking *smell* seems to sink into my bones. I close my eyes, and hit play on the answering machine. Bruce sounds sober as hell, but I hear the faint click of the red-hot cigar lighter biting through dried leaf.

"Hey. Have your fun but don't hit the booze too hard."

Seconds drag on.

"What I said at practice stands, but we had a good camp, remember. Checked in with the mechanics and they're loading the car up with some new goodies, full race trim and all. Our guys say Vesper's made some adjustments too, but not as much as us."

I crack my eyes open. It suddenly occurs to me that I might not have been off on any of the corners, if he refused to show me the footage. I hear him pause to take in some smoke.

"We got you where you need to be, and now you gotta forget about us— We ain't in that car with you. Can't wash out now, right? G'night."

Can't wash out.

Could I?

. . .

With an electronic *pop,* the answering machine turns off.

Can't Wash Out.

It's been August for so long that the trees simmer where they stand. The mossy coolness of the creek bed seems a good enough reprisal to us, more so than the A/C unit that blew a month ago that Dad still hadn't gotten around to fixing. Gregor had suggested bringing a pair of fishing poles with us, but in the cracked-mud heat the creek had receded and they lay forgotten on a moldering log. The pair of us sat on a lichen-riddled boulder in sticky silence.

"Was Dad mad when you told him?"

He chuckled. "Yeah. Glad I told you first, at least."

I brush some mud off of my knee, and bite out the question hovering above my head like the sword of Damocles. "Why'd you sign up, anyway?"

He spits off the rock. "I don't know. You saw the footage, what the Brazilians did to us, and what they wanna do seems pretty unforgivable."

"And dad?"

"And dad."

"I'm gonna miss you, Gregor."

"I gotta do this, Alex. We all gotta serve somehow. Can't wash out now."

And that was that.

He pulls me in for a hug that's unbearable in the shimmering heat and I hope it never ends. If I don't change the subject I will cry.

"What'd you do with your sign-up bonus?"

He grins, producing a pair of limp ticket stubs, holding one out to me.

"You're coming to this thing with me, just kicked off. You heard of the World Rally Tournament?"

I let that vision of sticky august afternoon drag me out of linen sheets and through the trash-strewn and abruptly empty streets of Cortez, the legion of rallygoers having retreated to the hills and to the course well before dawn. The route for the race we take will wildly differ from any of the practice sections, and will most definitely be more technical. Our guys snooped as much as they could but security has tightened in the waning weeks of the tournament and we have nothing but the notes officially provided to my Navigator. I nurse a cup of pitch-black coffee that's terrible, just terrible, like all coffee since the beginning of the War. It takes me a second to realize how hard I'm grimacing.

We pile out of the van and onto the gravel-strewn lot for final check-in. The air is pig-rich with the smell of burnt methanol, pungent and fruity. Overtuned engines tucked into garish liveries stutter and growl in idle: each car leaves ten minutes apart, making it nearly impossible to run into a rival on the course. I see two other cars, each with the accompanying army of mechanics, movable workshops, tents, and consultants. It takes an almost comical amount of manpower to drag a tournament-spec car to the starting line, but from there it's down to the driver and driver alone, as Bruce said. I tense and nearly drop my coffee as one of the remaining engine flutters to greater life, the thunderous report dissipating far into the low hills of the country as the car's wheels chew gravel and it speeds away. Your position in the rally is determined by your performance in practice, with the faster drivers later in the day. I silently acknowledge the chunky patchwork of blue and daisy yellow, traditional Vesper colors that seem to shine harsh through the thin layer of dust that coats everything this close to the trail. Charlie had me beat in practice, and the part of my mind that shirks the rally thinks it poetic he set his car up before me. I don't have time to dwell on it before Bruce cuffs me on the shoulder.

"Mechanics want a word with you before you send it."

It's harder to talk to him than I thought it would have been. I stare at the grooves and runnels in the gravel beneath my feet and nod to him offhand, ducking around him. I couldn't bring myself to even throw away the business card. It sits in my pocket like a hundred-pound weight. His leaden hand stays stuck where he put it, his voice carrying across the lot.

"What the fuck is your malfunction?"

"Just let me get in the fucking car."

I can feel the entire Vesper staff stop their work and turn to face us. The swirling visage of the bartender snaps into my mind's eye.

"This is what you signed up for. This entire seasons gone to shit if you can't keep your head on your shoulders."

Why won't he let me get in the car?

"I make myself clear, Alex?"

"Yes."

"You sure about that?"

"Yes."

"Don't fucking let it happen again."

My head feels full of cotton as I stumble-walk in the direction of my car. I barely nod a *thanks* to the mechanic that thrusts a carbon-fiber race helmet into my hands, but when a sweat-soaked mechanic matches my pace I'm forced to swim out of my fugue.

"Suspension actuators are running great, we ironed out the last of the kinks this morning. Fully remapped the engine computer and put on some fresh turbos, and we finally figured out how to run everything at reduced compression. We can push the turbos even harder, so the engine'll eat itself a few minutes after the predicted course time, so be careful," he warned.

"Good luck," he adds a moment later.

"Thanks," is all I can manage.

I slip the helmet onto my head and take a last breath of blast-heated California air before I step into the rally car. My rally car.

I find my office underneath a thin sheet of cherry red fiberglass stippled with sponsor's decals, vaguely in the shape of a line of passenger car that our parent sponsor sells. It's a well-known lie, aimed at cowing only the most gullible rallygoers into buying that car that won America the cup. The madness hidden just beneath that coat of paint bears absolutely no resemblance to any car on the road. The interior inside is a jungle-gym of spaced aluminum tubing, stripped to the bone. The passenger seat is entirely gone, the spot where the navigator would sit in the older days of rally now occupied by a carbon-tubbed tank of race-grade methanol that permeates the entire car with a pungent chemical tang that drowns out the smell of your own sweat. Everything is bespoke, designed for maximum performance in the few minutes it's required to work before the race is over and everything can be swapped, repaired, made right. I swing myself into the race-seat that was contoured to my own body lines and punch the ignition on button and revel in eager growl of the freshly tuned engine, slamming the shifter into first as the blood red digital indicator on the dash flashes from zero to one. I'm sitting in the reverberating chassis and waiting for the navigator's signal to *go!* When it occurs to me that the war, and the bartender, and Bruce are well out of my mind. My eyes are closed and the engine's idle has seeped into my bones when I hear the crackling shout of the navigator in my ear and I am off, all four wheels spinning, turbos fluttering.

The engine shrieks through four gears before I hit the first turn and I am dancing once again, the sheer force of tire-on-trail kicking a column of dust thirty feet into the air as I glide the car through the first gentle bends of the course with a quick flutter of the brake pedal. I see them now whipping by in the farthest corners of my vision in groups of twos and threes, the fans that had clogged the streets of Cortez all that time ago. The navigator cries in desperate warning as I rocket past a partially crooked tree almost perpendicular to the road, the all-encompassing hum of the turbos pushing me through the corner I barely had time to react to. I am too quick for my navigator. My breath slows and I put every ounce of my being into gliding on the rally car through each turn, concentrating on my navigator's frantic rambling and the slight give of the dusty trail.

I'm farther into the mountains and the pockets of rallygoers are only growing thicker; it doesn't take long to see the first of them scramble off of the edges of the trail as I scream past them. My heart stammers in my chest. *Nothing new. They can hear you coming. They know when to get out of the way.* I slam the shifter down two gears and the engine screams to and past the redline, the chassis groaning in protest as I take a second corner sideways, several of the fans almost making eye contact as I stand still for the heartbeat it takes to bleed my inertia into the dirt before I am blasting forward once more, the lag between my foot to the floor and the turbos flooding the engine with air impossibly more pronounced with the new setup. I see the phantom afterimage of tents in the periphery of my vision as I carve deeper into the trail, more and more fans on the course with every turn. It isn't long before a solid sea of them obscure the path ahead of me, parting ways in the final millisecond before my front bumper rushes in to meet them. I'm braking harder now, swaying in the dirt and slowing myself down as much as I dare to give the fucking fans more time to *move.* Whatever lies ahead is impossible to see in the undulating sea of bodies that covers the road. I set my teeth and listen even closer to the navigator.

Hard left, eighty degrees.

Soft Right. Don't cut. Sixty degrees.

Hard Right, one hundred degrees.

Continue straight.

. . .

—Shit! Bump ahead! Hard left!

The navigators words come at the same moment the sea of parting fans reveal the earth-hewn ramp directly in front of me. For the first time in the season, I send my brake pedal to the floor pathetically late. I lock the front and the rear of the car as hard as I can, grooved rubber slicing twin gashes into the loose-packed earth, wrestling for purchase with the wheel. I hit the apex of the ramp with the back end of the car sliding to the left, the force of jump continuing that motion until I am once more perpendicular to the course as I sail over the heads of the bravest rallygoers. I hang in the air for a moment, wheels spinning, engine reeling and then the trail is rising, rising to meet my where I float and I strike it with enough force to ablate the car's undercarriage and loosen the fillings in my mouth. Within the same instant my foot is to the floor and I'm sliding myself back into place, splaying the car out and taking the widest arc I can into the next turn. My mouth tastes of copper and the engine is howling to greater life as I lunge forward, fans falling back where they can, and—

There's a kid in the middle of the trail. Nothing is moving and it's happening all too fast and the turbos are buzzing to life and the kid is unmoved and uncaring of the cherry-red comet fast approaching. *They know when to get out of the way.* I ease off the throttle for a moment, and the split-second that decision gives me is enough time to get my bearings and strafe onto farthest banks of the trail, missing the kid by what has to be millimeters, and sliding back to the center.

I'm dimly aware of golf-ball sized rocks that festoon the edges of the worn dirt path, but whatever catches my right rear wheel has to be impossibly larger. The throaty snap of the entire wheel element tearing itself free seems to drown out every other noise in the car as the recoil of the impact rockets the left side of the car inwards, farther into the verdant border between trail and trees, the steering wheel twisting so violently I have no hope of holding on. My entire world seems to dip sideways, gnarled bark a millimeter away from the windshield.

My hands fly to my face as I tuck my head into my chest and wait for the indescribable impact that will arrive before my next heartbeat, eyes closed, breath drawn, *nothing.* Something is very wrong. I crack my eyes open and it takes my brain a long second to process the harsh glow of fluorescent lights and nondescript tiled floor. The headache hits me in the next moment, not so much a dull throb but a crisp sheen of agony that extends from my brow to the base of my skull. My teeth ache. Sitting next to my hospital bed is a chipped plastic tray holding what had to be the sole content of my pockets: The creased photo of my brother. It takes more than a second to stare at the faded lines of his face for my brain to fully process the kid, and the crash. The realization I'm out of the rally is so sudden that the photo falls out of my hands. I hug all that is left of my brother and mouth the word *sorry, sorry* until it doesn't have meaning. His words come back, *We all have to do something,* and I have no response. The cup will go to Vesper, and an American team will lose for the fourth year and counting. It's only after I set the photo back on the tray that I notice the folded business card wedged underneath. My heart skips a beat, but before I can process the torrent of memory flooding my cracked mind the only door into my room opens and Bruce walks in.

I'm breathing hard. *What if he somehow saw it?* My mind reels at the thought of what would happen to me, and all I focus on is keeping the rhythm of my breathing even. He's wearing aviators and chewing on something.

"Pretty nasty crash."

"Where am I?"

"Riverland Hospital. Impact woulda killed you if you hadn't braked so hard."

"Riverland?"

"Yea. Had you transferred a bit more than two weeks before the rally here."

A tension I wasn't aware I was holding seems to drain away. How am I still in the tournament?

"The Riverland rally? What's the point? Vesper beat me at Cortez, they have enough points over us to win the series no matter how Riverland goes."

"That's the thing. They didn't finish. You're still in it."

Bruce produces a camcorder tape from his back pocket, strolling over to the wall mounted television and sliding it into the adapter. Grainy footage from a tree-mounted camera displays Charlie's car ripping through the parting sea of spectators, kicking dust into the air and gently sliding through well-worn corners.

"Right here."

The car wavers, swaying gently on the trail and then losing it's footing all at once. My heart plummets in my chest as all I can do is watch the blue and yellow beast tumbles through the crowd far faster than they can react, bodies slamming into the car doors until Bruce casually hits pause, freezing the gash the car cut into the mass of rallygoers.

"The spectators pulled him out of the car after, beat him pretty bad. He'll live, but he's not racing at Riverland. Or ever."

I shudder as I think of the madness of those fans, the same that cheered for my victory or death in Cortez. All I can do is stare at him.

"I'm only gonna ask this once, because we gotta focus on getting you back on your feet for Riverland, but why'd you swerve?"

Riverland is suddenly the last thing from my mind.

"What?"

"Why'd you swerve? Spectators on the track has been a thing for years. They always move in time."

"Did you just see what Charlie did?"

He offhandedly shrugs.

"They always move in time when you don't crash."

"He was a kid!"

"How is this a mystery to you? You drive like they're invisible! You've been told this before!"

I have nothing to say to that. He keeps talking, suddenly calm.

"Just be ready for Riverland, sixteen days out. Like I said, Charlie's out and Vesper doesn't have a good enough replacement to challenge you. This is war, and we can take the cup home if we play our cards right."

"What? Brazil is a war! This is rally."

He shakes his head.

"What happened to you? Ever since that party in Cortez you've been all over the place, lost your spirit."

All I can think about is the business card. He doesn't know. The thought of punching those numbers into the first payphone I see, but the photograph next to it seems to slow my hand. The side of myself that is still with Gregor speaks up. *Don't do it for Bruce. Do it for Gregor. You can take that cup home, even with the crash.*

I check out of the hospital in the early evening and let the contents of my pocket pull me all the way into the hotel where my head aches and I stare at a gray ceiling so reminiscent of the hospital it makes me sick. I glance at the plastic phone for what has to be the hundredth time this night and finally, faster than I mean to, frantically dialing numbers and finally, finally holding the phone to my ear. My resolve holds out until

I first hear the slow beep of the call connecting and suddenly all I can think of is Gregor. Nothing but the faint crackle of call interference comes out of the receiver. I swallow hard as the seconds draw on. My hand is hovering an inch above the *terminate call* button when a faint voice most definitely belonging to the bartender, but touched by a rare kind of grief finally speaks.

"Turn on the radio, Alex."

I place the receiver on my bed and roll onto the other side, where it rests on a cramped nightstand. I don't have to be told to flip it to the news.

Almost in my head, I hear the faint whispers and gasps of the people in the rooms closest to me hearing what I'm hearing.

—announcement coming directly from the Commander and Chief of the United States armed forces, "it has become necessary, in the name of swiftly and absolutely ending the South American War, to fire a single nuclear-equipped missile at Sao Paulo. Retaliation is an impossibility. That is all."

The message loops back around.

Something seems to ache in my chest as I reach a hand out to flip the radio off. There's nothing left to hear from them. It takes the distant yet unmistakable sound of muffled clapping from the neighboring hotel rooms on all sides for me to finally pick the phone back up, the fact that my hand doesn't pass straight through it is somehow a shock. I need someone to tell me that what I listened to wasn't real, to explain how the government had cowed us all. I hear nothing on the line, and my thoughts are so loud it takes me a second I'm shouting them into the receiver.

"I need to win Riverland! Not for myself, not for this country, but for him! I promised him!"

. . .

"I know what I heard on the radio, but I've signed contracts. I can't just walk away from the Rally. And if I did it wouldn't help!"

I'm too tired to force myself to believe what I'm saying. Everyone, from the fans to the protestors to Bruce to myself seems to understand its existence, but just what the connection is seems an impossibility to understand. But that's why I'm on the phone, isn't it? The part of myself that admits how badly I wanted to know has finally won, no matter how much it could dash apart that perfect memory of my brother.

She finally speaks.

"I'm sorry."

I finally realize how hard I've been choking back tears.

"Thank you."

"You called because you wanted to know more. I can give that to you, but I can't promise you'll be ready for it."

"I am."

I can almost hear her smiling at me from the other end of the phone.

It doesn't take long for some unnamed figure to slide something underneath my door. I make no move to grab it until well after I hear their footsteps receding down the hall. My heart pounds in my chest as I creep across the room, gingerly lifting the manila folder and placing it on my bed. I switch the lamp on, and as a final nightmare of doubt flashes through my mind, I think of the inside of my car in the seconds before the start of the rally. I draw in a rattling breath, and flip the folder open.

I'm greeted by several meticulously photocopied papers, covered in neat roads of keyboarded words with cramped notes scrawled in the margins. I leaf through them and find a grayscale map of the world, showing the locations of every World Rally course: a sea of pinpricks in the states, like Cortez and Riverland, a lesser smattering across Europe, a few in north Africa, and several lone stragglers in Australia and mainland Asia. The notes in marker are far more interesting. Each course outside of the United States is dated to when it was constructed, along with the dates of trade agreements with America and the GDP growth of each country. The trends are startlingly easy to spot in retrospect: The popularity of the WRT has turned it into a weapon, no, a *gift* to be given out to the United States's chosen allies. The next sheet of paper I look at all but confirms it. The primary shareholders of the WRT are all inextricably linked to the highest echelons of the government, the President himself. I flash back to that bar in Cortez and feel slightly obtuse for not realizing then and there. *How does it connect to the war?* A news article that was obviously written in advance and left unpublished slides another puzzle piece into place. The title says it all: *Brazil agrees to build Basin Rally Course, host WRT.* I flip the paper over and scan the line of notes:

—Brazilian Government officials host secret meetings with WRT, decline to build course on their own dime even after threats of war . . .

—meeting is scrubbed from records and Brazilian officials are killed, Brazilian president was never aware.

—False flag attacks staged at south port by US to give official reason, immediate invasion follows . . .

Reading that page seems to both confirm the obvious and break my entire world in half. I feel myself sway where I stand. The war, the war my brother fought and died in was nothing but a retaliation against a country unwilling to host the madness of the WRT. I feel my head in my hands and for the first time I slide when I'm not in my car on dirt roads, I feel the entire world slide away from me. It's like my crash into the tree all over again, a total upending of any remaining stability in my world.

Almost without realizing it, I'm leaning on the hood of my brother's gently idling and thoroughly rusted out car, the sidewalls caked with mud. It's a day in infant September where the swirling late-summer heat has mellowed into a gentle warmth. The WRT event my brother had took me too had been weeks before, but the roaring engines of those mud-spattered cars had echoed around in my skull ever since. My brother had been more than happy to take me onto those untouched back roads closest to our house, eagerly letting me timidly guide his car through corner after corner.

"Make sure you keep up with this after I'm gone. You'll get it, in time."

My smile falters for a moment. I had forgotten his impending departure so easily on the trail.

"You thinkin' about doing the WRT someday?"

I laugh.

"You're joking right? I gotta long way to go before I'll even start thinking about that."

"I'm serious. You got plenty of time to get there, Christ, you're only fourteen and you're already on trails."

"Not very fast, though. I'll keep at it when you leave, promise. Every day."

He smiles. "I wanna see you on TV with that big silver cup in your hands, Alex. I know you can get it done."

The thought of being in those race-spec cars, shoulder to shoulder with the best drivers in the world is so daunting it makes me imagine what's going through my brother's head, watching the situation in Brazil slide further into chaos with each passing day. I'll take up a burden, same as him.

"I will, Gregor, I will."

We stand in soft silence for a moment.

"We should get going. Dad'll be mad."

"Sure, I got one last question, about the rally."

"Shoot."

"How do you get out of a slide?"

He shows his teeth.

"You floor it."

• • •

Without even realizing it I'm throwing the door to my apartment open and pacing down the carpeted hall, heading straight for the lobby. The receptionist lies asleep at his desk, his radio still gently repeating it's message from earlier in the night. The glass doors slide open with a slight squeak and I'm standing on the warm pavement of the parking lot, the hum of crickets all around. All of the mechanical equipment required to maintain the rally car, along with the car itself travels with us and the decaled trailer that holds the rally car I would have raced in Riverland stands solemnly in a forlorn corner.

I force the door open without much of a struggle, and suddenly I'm face to face with what perfectly resembles the car I crashed what feels like fifteen minutes earlier. The decals are even in the same place, but with the amount of damage I caused to the car it would have made more sense to rebuild the entire thing from scratch and throw away the ruined original. I'm barely taking the time to think of what I'm planning, operating off of pure instinct and throwing caution to the wind, exactly the kind of mindset sitting in the cockpit of the car in front of me forces you to take up. The twenty-gallon barrels of racing fuel are heavy, and hauling one across the length of the trailer makes the pain in my head sharply flare back to life, but once I begin to pour it once again subsides. The liquid is more pungent than I remember, with almost all of it winding up funneled into one of the cooling vents on the top and sides of the car. I realize I'm holding the matchbook I snatched from the hotel lobby with a clenched fist, my hands shaking so hard that it takes more than a minute to strike one of them alight.

I stare at the soaked car, and back at the gently wavering flame in my hands. Disappear from that hotel, never see Bruce or the rest of the team again, leave them nothing but the torched carcass of this car and yet another driver that did their part to end the madness, to stop the slide. I think of Gregor, and I no longer waver.

He was in over his head and he was trying to do right. He has no allegiance to the war you know of.

I smell the pungent, cherry odor of the methanol one last time.

I toss the match.

ABOUT THE AUTHOR

Oliver Stifel is a senior at Lower Merion High School and lives in Bala Cynwyd, Pennsylvania. In 2024 he was one of twenty students selected nationally to participate in the Alpha Young Writers Workshop. Oliver was chosen to be a

Writing Fellow at Lower Merion High School where he has served as a mentor to other students. He was recognized in Pennsylvania by representing his high school in the Central League Writing contest. An avid storyteller from a young age, Oliver plans to pursue a Bachelor's degree with a focus on English and Creative Writing.

Technicolor Bath

RAAHEM ALVI

I see you on the other side. Stardust. A strikingly blue supernova leaving drift tracks in my night sky. I want to tell you that I love you and to beg you to love me back. But I'm afraid I've become something you won't quite like.

"My biggest fear, huh? I guess my biggest fear is walking through my front door, seeing and not recognizing you. Then myself. Then the home I sit in and the life we're living. And having all of that coalesce into falling out of love with you."

"And when would this happen?"

Now. A maelstrom of tears swirled in her eyes. Words suffocated her throat as they swung in a spiral. A salty taste constant on her tongue from the tears slipping between her lips. Now. This is when she would fall out of love with her. Her pretty floret. Her shining comet across the skin of night. Her sweet princess. Neha wept.

"I still remember that day when my dad shit himself. I had to lie him on the bed, unbutton his pants and drag them off. It smelled horrible. Had to spray my room for hours on end. I bathed him and he kept crying. Just bawling his eyes. Crying and crying as I washed his behind."

"Did you hate him?"

"At that moment. I mean, it's hard to say."

"Be honest Neha, it's a judgment free zone."

Jetsam spirit and flotsam body. Dashed against stalagmites and stalactites. Neha watched Sumaira's once beautiful body hooked into wires and pipes. The *beep, beep, beep* in the room is incessant. An incubus had wrenched his arms around her throat, leaving her clawing and begging for oxygen. A hiss escaped with each heavy breath. Nozzles, fossils, beeps, torment. Apocalyptic, human-machine amalgamation. Her weak moist eyes and the pathetic desperation in her lungs. She could not recognize it.

"Love and hate are two sides of a coin. I was hating him out of love."

"So, heaven forbid, if I become old and decrepit, would you hate me out of love too?"

Sumaira, the catastrophe. Sumaira, the abject horror of flesh. Sumaira who sees the veil of reality. Sumaira, there is no more future. Sumaira, here there is only detritus and darkness. Neha touched Sumaira's feeble wrinkled mutilated hand. Her hissing voice bounced against the walls of her mask. Words were flung inside of her mouth, gargled and swallowed back. Little noises and creaks slipped through, with a slurry of saliva leaking through her lips. Meat-metal grotesquerie.

"I didn't hate dad. I don't think so. I hated the both of us. The permanent memory of my dad etched into my mind. I hated that. I hated the idea of what my dad had become."

"Old?"

"Not himself."

"He was himself."

"He wasn't what he always was."

"Will you hate me when I change and turn weak and pathetic?"

Neha wept her love from her eye sockets.

"Would you cry as much as dad?"

"Please find me. I see you in my dreams still. You're walking, dripping from head to toe, to my cottage because you swam to me. I'm dreaming again. All I'm seeing is you. I love you. Please love me again. Please find me in El Paraiso where I still see you in the skies."

Last words. 12:02am. Cassidy Newman. Sealed inside of a 9×12 inch envelope. Contents: a final invoice for a few thousand, instructions on insurance claims, an itemized bill upon request, condolences letter, data storage with a voice recording and billing instructions for acquiring more voice recordings. To be mailed to: Address Unavailable. No other available claimants.

On the other side of the wall, Neha sat in an office low lit. Surfaces of this space resembled black granite. Beside her, where sat large window panels, was the abyss. A sea vividly black with streams and streaks of luminescent white. She signed the paperwork. Contents: Terms & Conditions, congratulations letter, payment options and payment plans, contract with an expiration and her savings melted and imbued by ceaseless love. Her eyes crawled over the deposit invoice. A victim staring at the murder weapon. It was hanging above her throat now, waiting for the plunge. Love is a prison.

Neha sighed in El Paraiso. There it is in the distance, don't you see? Right there, off the highway. A collection of lances pointed skywards awaiting blast-off. Tear drop shaped towers ready to pierce the heart of a cosmic dragon. El Paraiso, the next step in human evolution. We preach oneness with all facets of the world, digital and organic. Our mission statement is the 140,_000 foot deep crater below filled with God's own black tears. This sea of tar and gasoline colored water is the blood from our hearts. This is who we are: El Paraiso, your bestest friend in death. Think of us as death and the black sand beaches as your vapid old life. Here it is, the ultimate destination. And we will grab God by the throat and bleed him dry.

At El Paraiso, the black sea is our war of attrition. Float with us or fall overboard.

"I hope you understand the service, Miss Ahmed. The Transference process does not copy nor simulate consciousness. It is a destructive process that transfers human consciousness into our cloud storage. We will create a 3D map of Sumaira's nervous system and brain, taking snapshots of her brain layer from layer. After that synthetic neurons will be introduced into Sumaira's brain which will remove organic neurons and create a map of her neural pathways. The combination of those neurons and the 3D digital structures will be used to transfer Sumaira's consciousness into El Paraiso's cloud storage. Legally, Sumaira will still be considered human though she will require new identification. Going forward, you will be considered Sumaira's legal guardian."

A legal document sits in front of Neha, staring at her with warnings and threats. Neha's eyes scurried and darted from word to word.

"You cannot request deletion of Sumaira's consciousness once the transfer happens. Deletion is classified as murder under new federal laws. Sumaira can request deletion in accordance with local bylaws. Upon failure to pay, Sumaira's consciousness will be frozen within the cloud storage until all invoices are fulfilled."

All of these words darted from corner to corner of the room as repellent molecules. Atoms collided and settled in her mind as mangled interpretations of whatever was said. There was a whirlpool in her mind. Little is of matter at this time. Neha is floating. Let her float. Stop rocking the raft.

"Sumaira will be available for a conversation within the coming week. The process of transference can be disorienting and distressing. She may struggle with the lack of movement and dissociation. Her first week in El Paraiso will be spent doing exercises with our coaches. They will do daily tests with her to see how she is adjusting. We will monitor her mood and her mental health. We will make sure she gets used to her new body. We can also edit her personality to suppress negative emotions and enhance positive ones. There will be a fee but we offer a dynamic payment plan."

Neha's thoughts had long been drowned in the bottomless black. El Paraiso, the abyssal plain. El Paraiso, the deep dive. El Paraiso, no life here, no oxygen. El Paraiso, the crushing weight of isolation reigns here. Everything that hurts is here and nowhere else. Nuke the pit, dehydrate it, terraform it, launch it into the closest quasar cluster.

"I have read the report. The accident was terrible, Miss Ahmad. I'm sorry that you had to see your wife go through this. Please rest easy and know that you made the best possible decision. We will give her a second chance and a happier, painless life."

Neha was cruising in the bottomless pit. On autopilot. Wavering in the currents and torrents of sentience. Nothing here but us and detritus.

"Where are you? Annie, where are you? I'm seeing you sitting in front of me but you never speak to me. I know it's not you. It's something different. It's terrifying me. Even if you don't say anything to me, please just sit in front of me once again. Please don't leave me here. I'm waiting for you in El Paraiso. And you're the universe. There's nothing here but you. Please. Please love me again."

Last words. 3:02am. Prakash Kapoor. The hard drive is fried, the software reset. There's no humans here, only planktons. And even they wonder if they exist or are they just a fragment of God's stray wild imagination.

"Do you remember your dad's final days, Neha?"

"Of course. He was standing at God's door, knocking. God was taking his time to come open it. He left him out in the rain, screaming all day for his mama. And I washed him. Fed him. Cleaned his shirts when he puked."

"Did you hate him?"

"I hated the circumstances. Like God, this man raised me. I wanted to run away. He was puking on my memories of holding me in his arms. Fuck. He didn't remember me. I would've preferred it if I only had to stand at the funeral, cry and get over it in a year or so. He didn't leave me with enough stamina to even muster a tear."

"It sounds like you hated him."

• • •

Neha positioned herself in a white cubicle. In front of her sat a touch pad with a storage port. She uploaded the photos of her apartment into it. Processing. Processing. Her memories of home bled into the walls and slowly coated each corner of her cubicle creating a facsimile. Their collection of records. Random assortment of posters they bought to coat holes in their cheap rental unit. A window framed by flora cradling within its sights a city brutalist gray. Rain caressing the skin of glass.

"What's important now, Miss Ahmed, is that you support her. We need to establish normalcy in Sumaira's life. It's a transitional period. She may feel scared and easily fatigued. We have edited aspects of her personality so this mood won't last long. She will feel home soon enough. Here is a list of words and topics you should avoid. We emphasize that despite any errors, glitches or any other occurrence, you continue your conversation as if nothing has changed."

Sumaira's randomly dispersed collection of themed rubber ducks and clown dogs. Sumaira's coat, bras, T-shirts distributed over each tile in organized chaos. Music is in the air. Love is in the air. The tiles each carry little pockets of the abyss within fractal divisions. Let's not stare there too long, Sumaira. My eyes the radiance of many moons in the night and every deep bright combination of quasar and starlight. Eyes here.

Neha had felt that, subconsciously, she had created a script for this moment. But now, as the computer in front of her (with a curved monitor and an 85mm camera staring down on her as God's eye) booted open, that script flushed itself deep inside the recesses of a netherrealm in her mind. Different terrifying and uncomfortable dialogue boxes and windows booted open in front of her, popping in and out of existence. And then—a photo. Sumaira. Sumaira, the computer. Sumaira, the undead. Sumaira, not here.

"Your current package does not include a 3D reconstruction of Sumaira's body. But we are able to upload a photo into our system, and then our AI specialists will have it animated and correspond to words Sumaira says. It will be exactly like having a video conversation."

Sumaira's cool crystal eyes were locked into Neha's. Neha smiled.

"Sumaira, can you hear me?"

Her lips parted.

"I can, Neha. Are you there? Can you hear me?" replied a voice deep and masculine.

"Our AI will take some time to absorb and recreate Neha's voice based on the recordings you have provided. The process can be expedited though.

It isn't a part of your current package but we can discuss this more if you'd like. Otherwise, for the first week, we will be using a placeholder."

"Neha?"

"Yes, my love."

"Are you there, princess?"

"Of course I am, baby."

"We did it, Neha."

"Yeah. We're still together."

"I know. I love you, my princes."

"I love you too, Summi."

"I'm just happy I can speak to you again. There were so many things I wanted to say to you but I couldn't. But now I can. Neha. My Neha. My beloved Neha. I'm so happy I can say your name again!"

Neha smiled. Despite the constant radioactive combustions on her heart and the draw of the abyss in her mind, she was happy in this second. "I wish I could hold your hands" was the next thought that passed her mind. And, as it passed, it left behind a nuclear fallout.

"Full reconstruction of her body is an option in our Platinum package. We will use a combination of synthetic and organic products to give Sumaira the perfect shell. Unfortunately Miss Ahmed, based on your provided statement, you are ineligible for this package at this time. You may have options if you have a guarantor. We do offer cheaper packages where Sumaira can use existing shells within our cold storage. We are unable to guarantee her appearance though."

"Existing shells? You have spare shells sitting around?"

"Oh yes! Sometimes clients are unable to fulfill invoices so we are forced to claim the shells back."

Love is in the air. And below the feet sits a great drawing abyss.

"I guess I'm at the age where I'm always thinking of death. How will I die? What will survive me? What am I leaving? It's just that time. Just that place. I feel that every second my bones crack and I lose my hair. It hurts now when I breathe. I've thought about it multiple times. I am the memories I leave behind me. I don't want to leave you memories of me degenerating. I want you to remember the person you loved."

Neha paused the recording.

"That was beautiful, Neha."

"Was it?"

"Yes. An art project, you said?"

"Yeah. I was recording my dad's last days. Titled *Degeneration*. Him trying to survive on his paycheck."

"He was a driver, right?"

"Yeah. This was the intro."

"What happened to the rest of it?"

"I scrambled all of the footage when he died. Symbolic gesture. Performance art."

Electric eels and bioluminescent stardust. Swimming and cruising in a digital broth. Sumaira's unblinking existence was stuck as a snapshot of time. Here moves no grains of sand nor does the detritus reach the abyss. Here, where catastrophe sleeps as a solemn transhumanist horseman of apocalypse, there is a distant light of aquatic life. Its light is a mockery of Sumaira's stillness. It is blinking now.

Sumaira, the numbness. Sumaira, the blue of the night sky is fading into a vivid black. The darkness is the coming of the apocalypse. Sumaira, we are going overboard and will become stardust.

Sumaira felt herself becoming a memory of herself. A living recollection. The stillness of existence through the camera had left her fading in and out. No dreams here nor starlight, only anemone.

"Dreaming requires extra computational data and capacity. It is the result of chaotic stochastic brain processes that can, sometimes, cause issues within our computational systems. There are certain packages available but they will cost—"

Sumaira, unblinking. She realized what she had been missing. She had left behind in the waking world a tinge of sadness and blues. Her mind was in constant nonconsensual happiness. But the words never came.

Neha never came. But Sumaira's coach sat in front of her. Her old mouth flung at Sumaira words she thought she understood. There were no contexts. There were no sums. There was only consumption then response. She hadn't felt the words wade in her sea of consciousness before sinking inside and drowning in the digital broth. No, the words had struck her skull and left a dent.

"Are you adjusting well Sumaira?"

"I'm not feeling myself."

"That's totally alright. You're adjusting to the way the computer allows you to think. Your thoughts, unlike before within your human nervous system, are linear and precise. Your thoughts have added reference and context from our directory and repository of data."

"My thoughts aren't my own?"

"Absolutely not the case. The data is what you find. The thoughts are the conclusions you make."

"I don't feel myself thinking. I don't feel much of anything."

"Feeling is an experience associated with organic human senses. Feeling is a bit different digitally. Your consciousness will perceive colors and codes which imitate warmth, happiness, love. You're still getting used to it. You're still feeling. It's just different. We will keep doing exercises, okay?"

"Okay."

"Now, when I say love, what do you feel?"

Neha's face appearing in the lines of codes. Neha's name imprinted on every node. Neha is every feeling and every last touch with the waking world. Love. Love is associated with a face that is specifically desired. L-O-V-E- defined as the thing that I need in here. Love. Something I cannot taste or smell nor touch. It is what I see. And I see Neha. She must be that thing called love.

Sumaira, here, where the veil between reality is thickest. And everything that was ever loved is a stardust speck's shadow. And things said are unfelt under the sheet of 62126.2 psi saltwater pressure. Here, at the bottom of the abyss.

"I'm feeling myself becoming a memory, Neha. Your father is all alone now. Xavier died a month ago. Good man. Last one. I was always afraid of being the last one. The world has grown so much faster than me. I don't recognize it. It's not my world. I'm not supposed to be here. I've outlived my time. I'm stuck here in a pocket of time, left behind by everyone in the universe."

Things here lurk and skate across the seabed. Scared of the light. Spend too much time behind the veil and sunlight becomes the enemy. The waking universe is an illusion behind the glass, silken and sweet. Sumaira had felt the consequence of dreamless and sleepless nights start sinking. Neha seemed an illusion. Neha seemed a dream. Everything on the other side of existence was a lucid dream, and her own voice was an enigma. Her lips spat lines of singular, one dimensional thoughts. Patterned thinking. Circles and triangles. Flat, 2D shaped surface neurological reality. Zombie parasite consciousness.

"Neha, I haven't felt human in a while."

"What do you mean?"

"The sum of all parts that make things human. I feel something different. Like I'm grasping at straws to make things come together wholly. But I feel like I'm consuming reality as little parts of a puzzle—and the rest of it is missing. Nothing is coming together. And I can't feel sad at it. I want it to feel sad. I can't. And it's hurting me."

"I mean, Miss Ijazi, who are you talking to? Neha isn't here."

Misery is #739B3. She knows she feels for the reality in her camera has desaturated and been reduced to simple shape blocks of #739B3.

Existence is one large Rothko. Little speckles of colored light given form, function, meaning, power, misery by senses wholly organic, universal and supernatural. Inference to the divine carried in every piece of bent light. Here, within the abyss, existence was a stasis. Everything was conscious input and output.

"Your consciousness, Sumaira, is the sum of three parts. Architecture, Process, Behavior. APB. The physical construction of your brain and the cross-level interactions between its different parts. The cognitive processes within your brain, from interactive to dormant. The emergent behavior from these processes and architecture. Consciousness is how the world acts upon the sum of these three parts and your response to it. We exist as an answer in the context of a societal question."

"What is that question?"

"The question resonates in everyone's heart. How we interpret it is an effect of our different neural pathways. I have felt the question. You have felt the question. Consciousness is an adaptation by evolution to answer that question."

The question is: When will Neha visit me next? That is the universal question. That is what everyone feels and asks.

"What if you don't know the question?"

"The question is a fundamental aspect of Homo sapiens existence, Miss Ijazi. It is the building block of all that is true. It is sentience manifest. Everyone feels the question."

Sumaira, the bottom of a bottomless sea is where the question sits. A monstrous presence is perverting its shape and form, but the question is still there.

"Am I real?"

"Each night I see black holes burst and evaporate. Trails of drifting light expelled from their disks. I still see them. Here I am. All alone. I and little specks of light that never reach my eyes. Reality is the few sun bursts I see through the veil. Everything else is REM sleep. And I am beginning to see that I was always dreaming. I never once awoke."

Last words. 4:05 am. Maryam Ahsan. No time left. Reality is floating in a sunbeam. Reality is ensnared inside of a flesh shell. The shell is gripping it with a rigor mortis. Existence is a jetsam comet adrift in the skin of night.

Sumaira saw photos of her brain scan that night. Some part of her gray matter, at a molecular level, was pixelated. The resolution. The resolution killed a part of her. The translation of her brain, cells, tissues, neurons and their connectivity into their digital model was fucked from the start.

A little indolent piece of gray matter.

"Neha."

"Yeah."

"You're only doing this because you hate yourself for hating me."

"Do you think I hate you, Summi?"

"I know you."

Neha's mind had been wandering into the same violent crevices inside her mind. Each little jagged and ragged line in her brain asked the same loud question: "I don't know whether to kill myself or you."

"Mama and Baba won't see me?"

"This is still blasphemy to them. They're adamant that this is all a violation of Allah's design."

"But their imam's luxury car isn't."

Neha wanted her so badly. Every atom in her being craved Sumaira. Her lips. Her eyes. Neha's eyes remained locked with Sumaira's 3D model. The model was under a light resembling the room's. Every pore and every texture was accurate to Summi's face. Except the gaze. The monitor filtered out the sexiness of her glare. It was cold now. Empty. It was weightless when it once carried the universe on her eyelashes.

"You didn't come see me, Neha."

"I was busy."

"You were scared."

"What makes you say that?"

"Because the current me is a spit on the person you loved."

Neha's mind reverberated that same thought. *I don't know whether to kill myself or you.* Cornered by love. No way out without embarrassment or disgust. No specks of light breaking the surface of the water anymore. Only us and detritus. No one will have to live with this shame. Sinking vessel. No more kids in the rooms. It was the cold that killed you. It was the photon sphere and the blazing disk of a jetsam quasar that killed us. Here there is only the event horizon and past it, love is stretched into a metaphor.

"It was 7:00pm. I was sitting in our living room. I've put everything that belonged to you in our bedroom. I've been sleeping on the couch so I wouldn't run into your things. I was sitting there and, on the TV, all of your streams were still there. I saw the last movie you watched. You didn't get to finish it. 'Latest picks for you.' I felt like you never left. That you were still here, sleeping next to me. It sunk in finally. You're not here, Summi. I missed you too much. I miss you."

"I'm still here, Princess."

"No. No you're not, Summi."

Sumaira did not know what was her. Sumaira was the reflection in the mirror and the descriptions of other people. Here, where there is a projection and here where description is quantitative, Sumaira had become null.

I am just neural pathways.

I am energy combustion.

"It's five in the morning. It's Summi's birthday today. I have a little trip planned for us. She wanted to go to that dog concert. It sounds fucking stupid but whatever. I love her. She's my idiot. And, of course, the idiot wants fast food for dinner. She better not think that's how my birthday will go. I'm expecting fine dining—something premium. At least I can spend some money on her gift. She asked me to get her this fancy pebble. Wallahi, I will and I'll beat her with it."

Sumaira had been given access to a virtual cafe. Trial run. A 3D space. 3D body. Touch and smell here were so visibly inputs and outputs and computationally calculated sensory experiences that she felt overloaded.

The scent of coffee, the low roar of crowd conversations, the blinding whiteness of the windows. She found herself a little corner. Corners were safe. Nothing fits in a corner and nothing can jump out from it. Vantage point.

The seat felt different against her body. The pressure of sitting felt different. The touch was all wrong. It wasn't going in the right place. Her whole body vibrated from the motion and sensor. She closed her eyelids. She parted them. And in front of her, in her goth make-up, white dyed hair and deep black mascara sat Neha. Neha wore that tight fitting dress that she had on their first date. Sumaira remembers that night. Ah, Aphrodite herself had fallen into her grasp. Every curve was perfection.

"You're not Neha."

"Who really is Neha?"

"What do you mean?"

"Who is she really? Personality types? Phenotype? Genotype? Neurons and microtubules? Germs and cells? Calcium and marrow? Is she the tapeworms inside her stomach? Is she the coffee addiction? Is she the mascara and black lipstick? What is Neha?"

Neha is the grounding node within a dream. Neha is El Paraiso.

"Neha is a thing that is recognized as Neha and cared for as Neha."

"And when Neha becomes a thing that is neither."

"She is still Neha."

"Have you ever loved Neha? Or did you love the little whispers of, 'look how lucky she is' whenever you showed up at parties and bars?"

"I loved Neha for everything that she was and everything that she brought me."

"You loved Neha for how she chemically reacted to you. Do you love Neha the object or Neha the universe?"

The universe. The missing element.

"Humanity is the universe filtered through your consciousness. Humanity is the reaction of the universe to your sentience and your reaction back into its emptiness. There are no questions here. The universe does not act upon this construct. This is emptiness and you are a vacuum given sentience. There is nothing here, Summi. You're swimming. Time has crushed us into dust."

Her humanity is a tomopteris sinking into crushing depths.

"Things here are interwoven by gossamer threads. Galaxies. Quasars. Everything is connected by thinly woven strings of living systems. Humanity is connected by thinly woven strands of gravity. Each human is connected by senses. Perception. Scent. Self. These create the gravitational web which locks all of us into complex zooids. Countries, cities, villages. Everything is a zooid cluster. Our little family is a zooid. Consciousness is the wax which gels this zooid cluster together. Your mom, I and you, Neha. We together are a unit that creates a zooid. Our house is a living system."

Love is the gossamer threads of consciousness intertwining and knotting into a singular thread. Love is Sumaira and her skin glistening with layers of moisturizers at midnight. The tip of her nose is shining. Lips are craving to kiss every inch of her face in her sleep. Sumaira, she will never know how much love she is shown in her sleep, within the tightness of the arms, with warm kisses against her cheek. Sumaira, I don't know how to love you this way. Sumaira, you were better off dead so I wouldn't feel this way.

Sorry.

"In a way you're right. I suppose, you are two people, Miss Ijazi," the coach replied to Sumaira, "there is the brain that was there before and the brain that exists as a 3D web inside the Cloud storage. There is psychological continuity between the you before and the you after yet both exist as separate entities. It doesn't mean that you're not the same person. It just means that there are two occupants in your consciousness. The old you and the new you."

"There was one that died."

"No, they both survived and live within you."

"No. Sumaira the organism died. The one that carried me within its shell. She was left behind inside of a flesh suit."

"These are philosophical perspectives, Miss Ijazi."

"She is dead. And I'm the one left behind."

"Miss Ijazi, the organism is an animal. It is not human. Humanity is your thoughts. Humanity is a psychological phenomenon. When you proclaim your humanity, the one speaking is you, not the organism. The organism is a host for your consciousness. Everything that comprises the sum of all parts of your humanity is here in El Paraiso."

"The organism is the one who felt Neha. The organism is the one who wanted to make love to her. The organism is the one who craved her lips and her tongue. I just showed it how and kept the conversation going. And Neha, the organism, is the one who wanted Sumaira. The organism is gone. She doesn't recognize me."

Here it was. It's coming back now. Personality edits and adjustments be damned. Isolation is an inevitability. Here it was, the equilateral triangle of love: hatred, pain, frustration.

"I am sinking Neha. Please hold me."

"Miss Ijazi?"

"Neha, I am sinking."

All things that exist within humans exist within the universe. So does intelligence. So does pain. So does isolation. So does love. So does hatred. So does Neha.

"Neha, there will come a point that I won't be your father anymore. Whatever I am will be gone. The creature in front of you will be restless and loveless. Please love him like you loved me. For my sake, love him. We all need love. Love comes from the universe, Neha. It is a blessing from Allah. Please love him so he dies being loved."

Floating in the cosmic soup of existence. Bubbling temperatures. Raspberry tastes. El Paraiso, where things come to be separated from the universe. Where every neural spark is a nuclear explosion.

Sumaira, things fell apart. Sumaira, I cannot love anymore. Sumaira, here is every bit of warmth in this heart so let me unlove you. Let this be the last time I see you hurt the memory of you.

El Paraiso, the human mass stranding. Rotting consciousness. The end.

"Neha."

"Yeah?"

El Paraiso, the midnight zone between tomorrow and after. No more tickets to the afterlife. Here things are left stranded till the heat death.

"Please tell me you love me."

"I love you."

El Paraiso, meat locker for drained and emptied organs.

"Mean it."

"I loved you."

Neha's eyes locked with the animated photo. No more 3D models. Little to no money in the bank. Empty loveless, pitiless eyes. Brutalist gray granite concrete block eyes. A gaze that crashed into the lens rather than swim inside. Effervescently cruel look.

Sadness appears as a cyanosis on the skin of reality.

"I need a little more love from you right now, my baby."

"What do you want, Summi?"

At the end of the universe there are no explosions, no lights, no energy, no combustion. It is a silent evaporation. The universe dies quietly. The heart breaks with no splendor. No fireworks. No explosions. No nukes set off. Heartbreak is #739B3.

"I want to die."

Heartbreak is a silent tectonic shift. Consequences unfelt. I'm already dead. Super seismic distortion. Specks of light are puncturing holes in the darkness at the surface of the water. Microbes are scattering.

"I will be a color in the night sky, Neha. I will be a star dust. I'll be up there. It's all people up there. You'll be watching me."

El Paraiso, where she said goodbye.

"Last night I told Sumaira I love her. Dunno what I was thinking. Thinking to myself now and have been for a while: What did I mean? What does 'love' mean? What did she hear and what did I tell her? I'm guessing that word means something different for everyone. I don't know what I meant though. I guess what I was trying to say is that she makes me feel real."

Neha, the isolation of the universe has become ever so vast. Dark energy surrounds our little human shaped islands and the closest cosmic body drifts further and further. As months pass, their lights will vanish and become a memory. And then the last person who remembers the stars will die. Then there will be no stars ever. They will fall out of existence.

Miseries and happiness will wash away as time erodes lifetimes. Specks of light will break though the surface until the water is all dried. Contract killer. Family annihilator. Death bringer. Sweet lover. The universe will explode. And a ripple will send all planktons scurrying.

Neha, here, at the bottom of the sea of consciousness, the netherrealm, there is a thing sleepless and restless. It is gargantuan.

Neha, here, in the room where your universe died there are still echoes of love. The energy has seeped into the tiles. Stay here, where all things that hurt exist and all things that love existed.

Neha lied back. And pressed play. Then rewind. Her proposal beachside, on a black sand dune, where Sumaira's mother tripped from excitement. Sumaira's screams and yelling. Neha's dad's ceaseless clapping. When things were recognizable.

Neha realized that time had made her a stranger to the universe. A different sort of loneliness sank in her heart. No one who recognized her in the ways she was recognized remained. She then became a stranger to herself.

At the isolation of 12:00am, Neha drove into the midnight.

Night cruising and waiting for the world to become less stranger.

Things here come to the waking world stranded and dying. Humans are washed on shore from the cosmos. She would return one day to the skies and become star stuff.

Together again they would be colors.

ABOUT THE AUTHOR

Raahem Alvi is a Pakistani-Canadian writer, artist and a lover of all things related to science, cosmic eldritch abominations and good food. When he's not writing, he's either wearing his wrists out from extremely intricate ink drawings or hanging out with stray cats.

Unquiet Graves

MICHAEL SWANWICK

The wind doth blow today, my love,
And a few small drops of rain;
I never had but one true-love;
In cold grave she was lain.
—Anon.

George Massey drove up the twisty roads of Granite Hill Cemetery with a fresh new body in the trunk of his eCar. At the foot of the hill the oldest graves, slate and sandstone softened by centuries of rain, dated back to colonial times. The stones grew larger with altitude, climaxing in Victorian mausoleums large enough for a man to live in, rows of granite obelisks, and ponderous memorials topped by weeping angels or draped urns. They were carved with names and dates and, very rarely, a pious sentiment that revealed nothing about the person buried there. He didn't bother stopping to read any of them. Here, the dead never spoke, and what he needed to hear no living soul could tell him.

He parked at the highest point of the cemetery and got out. From this vantage, he could look down on all of Port Hebron and a slice of the moon-silvered Mantowagan that was the reason for its existence. His entire life was encoded in the circuitry of its streets. Down there behind the firehouse was where he had smoked his first cigarette and over in the scrub woods by a bend in the river was the unofficial lovers' lane where he had lost his virginity—lost? thrown scornfully away!—three days after getting his driver's license. Over by the high school was Township Park where, one strange and wonderful evening, he and Jenny had sat on the playground swings talking, talking, talking as dusk turned into night and then kissed for the first time.

At the thought, Massey turned away and started walking downhill. He wanted the exercise, and he could always summon his car when he needed it.

The obelisks and mausoleums grew fewer and the gravestones less grandiose as he descended into the twentieth century and beyond. His handheld beeped. "Cerebral stent," it said aloud. Then, "Stomach cuff. Stomach cuff. Titanium alloy hip. ID chip: Herbert Vanderhocht." Massey paused to read the grave:

HERBERT V. B. VANDERHOCHT JR.
JANUARY 14, 1956 – DECEMBER 22, 2041

Herbert had died in his eighties. So the chip had probably been implanted to help recover him if he wandered away from assisted living.

Massey walked on. "Immunocompromised—do not perform surgery without downloading specifications and directives," his handheld said. And, a little farther, "Served in the United States Marine Corps. Lance Corporal, honorable discharge. Veteran of the First Brazilian War, Purple Heart." Then, "This individual has been genetically optimized. Physical responses acceptable for unoptimized patients may indicate serious impairment." Voices murmuring about him, Massey descended through a stratum of cemetery where every last corpse retained a complete medical history which he could read if he wanted to. He did not want to.

The stone monuments gave way to repurposed metals and multicolored replastics. Bluegreen foxfire flickered before some and faint spirit lights came and went above others. That had been a fashion of the times. In cemeteries less conservatively regulated than Granite Hill, the equivalent sections flashed and sparked like knee-high Times Squares.

Massey stopped by a familiar stone and tapped on his device.

"*Who dares summon me from the vasty depths of Hell? Who is so cruel as to torment this damned soul with memories of life and chances forever lost?*"

He couldn't help smiling. "You always make that same joke, Dad."

"Because it's timeless, Son. The best jokes are always a little corny. Also, I should have splurged for a top-of-the-line personality bead. This one's kind of limited."

"You've got all the personality in the world, Pops."

"As if that were a compliment. All kidding aside, I may be a pale shadow of the man I was when I was alive, but I'm not stupid. You've been dropping by pretty much every night. Let me guess. On your way to see Jenny?"

"Yeah, I . . . I have some things to go over with her."

"How's that going for you?

"Not so hot. We weren't getting along very well toward the end."

"I know. I was there. Upload me onto your handheld, kiddo. Maybe I can help. I know stuff you don't."

"Dad, I'm good."

"You know what Einstein said? Insanity is doing the same thing over and over again and expecting different results. I don't know what you're up to but it's obviously not working. Give me a chance."

Massey hesitated, then snapped, "Sure. Fine. Whatever." He waved the handheld at his father's grave, and crammed it back in his pocket. "Anyway," he muttered, "tonight I brought the body."

As they walked downhill, Massey's father shared monologues from the memorials they passed.

"I died a virgin. My parents thought that was important, I don't know why. I asked them once and they never visited my grave again. I got good grades in school. I liked playing Hen Quest and Unicorn Valley but—can you keep a secret?—Boy Band was my rave. Sometimes I think about all the stuff I missed out on."

Then: "He was my life, my love, my everything. I outlived him by thirty years and forgot his name long before I died. I begged and begged but my bastard children wouldn't pay for the upgrade that would restore my memories of him. May they rot in Hell forever for that."

Then: "I led a quiet, inoffensive life. Perhaps that's why, as I lay dying, I regretted every second of it."

"Dad, this is depressing the heck out of me."

"Of all sad words of tongue and pen, the saddest are these: It might have been. John Greenleaf Whittier. Don't let that happen to you. Get out there and grab life by the horns."

"That's what I'm doing right now."

"In a cemetery? At night? When you could be out dancing? Or, I don't know, boosting cars? Don't answer that, we've arrived. There's her grave."

They came to a modest stone marker reading GENEVIEVE GREENE MASSEY. For a long moment, Massey stood silent before it, composing himself, readying his arguments. He threw his head back to take in the starry sky above and the trees silhouetted black before it. When the moment felt ripe, he—

"Well, if you're not going to speak, I will. Hello, Jenny."

"Second Daddy! What a pleasant surprise. What's your life like? Did you ever get that boat you wanted? Still driving the girls mad? Tell me everything."

"I'm dead. The old ticker gave out a couple of months after you died."

"I'm so sorry."

"Don't be. We're all headed toward that same destination and more arriving every day. Also, as you know, being dead's not all that bad. The grave's a fine and private place, even if none do here embrace. Except teenagers. They're the bane of my existence. You'd think my plot was the only patch of grass in the state, the way they—"

"Ahem," Massey said.

There was a moment's startled silence. "Oh. You brought George."

"I had no choice. He's the one with the gizmo. I'll tell you what, though. It's kind of a kick getting into a new section of the cemetery, hearing stories I haven't heard a thousand times before. It reminds me of all the time I spent in dive bars listening to broken down old lushes ramble on."

A rush of wind ran up the hillside, accompanied by a brief spatter of rain. Then all was still again. "Listen to that!" Jenny said. "I miss rain so much. Are the first drops still accompanied by a touch of cold air? Does the smell of the earth still rise up to your nostrils? Is there just the slightest tension in the air, almost like a tingle of electricity?"

"There's only one way to find out," Massey said.

"George, no! Stop. We've already talked this to death. It's not going to happen. I made my choice and that's that."

"If you'd only listen to reason, we could—"

"Cut! Time out!" Massey's father cried. "Retreat to your corners and don't come back out fighting until you've told the baffled old dead guy what it is you're talking about."

Massey looked down at his wife's grave, up at the sky, back down again. He took a deep breath. "I guess the best way to explain it is to show you." He summoned his car. When it slid to a stop before him, he told it to open the trunk.

The body within was female, young, pretty. It wore sneakers, jeans, T-shirt, and a light jacket.

"It's a cherry," he said. "Factory new, never been ridden." With a touch of bitterness, "Nothing but the best for my sweetie."

"Son, not that it bothers me ethically, scandalous old reprobate that I am. I mean, look at my life. But what you're obviously planning to do is very, very illegal. You should take that into account. You get one shot at resurrection, immediately after you die, and if you opt out, that's it. Jenny made her choice. How are you going to explain her being back again?"

The body climbed out of the car and came to stand by Massey, perfectly expressionless. He patted its cheek. "Look at this face. It's nothing like Jenny's. I'll just tell everyone I got a new girlfriend. We can take up where we left off."

"Dream on, George. I like being dead. It's quiet, peaceful, drama-free . . . Everything that being married to you wasn't. Who are you to drag me back?"

"I'm the guy who took big risks getting this body for you. It cost me a bundle. I had to dodge the Feds and that wasn't easy. I worked nights to pay for it all. And you know why? Because I love you, that's why."

"Love. You wouldn't know love if it bit you on the butt. I had this argument with you how many times when I was alive? It's—oh, the hell with it. Just go away."

As happened every time they talked, Massey felt anger rising up white-hot within him. Always before, it had ended with him slamming into the car and driving away. Tonight, however, he was determined to embrace it and make it work for him. "You always say that. But you know what? I'm not asking your permission anymore."

"Son, you're making a big mistake here. I've done my best to protect you but—"

"Shut up, Dad." Massey jabbed an access code into his handheld and launched a capture-and-install app that had cost him dearly on the BlackNet.

The body standing beside him threw back its head and took a convulsive gasp of air as Jenny's persona was slammed into place.

"Don't talk." Standing behind Jenny, Massey gripped her shoulders with both hands. "Just listen to your senses. What do you see? What do you smell and hear?"

"I . . . I see the moon. It's so bright!" Wisps of clouds turned white as they crept by it, darkened as they left. "I can smell the leaves, starting to change and fall and turn to mulch. Listen! That sound in the distance—a train whistle? Or is it a werewolf howling? Maybe it's a lost soul being hauled down to eternal damnation, screaming all the way."

"That's my little girl. You were dead so long you forgot how much you loved life. But I knew that once you got a taste of it again—"

Jenny turned to face Massey. Smiling, she punched him hard in the stomach.

He doubled over in pain.

When he could speak again, Massey said, "What the hell was that for?"

Eyes blazing, Jenny said, "This is my body now? Well, you put something inside it after I explicitly told you not to. I call that a violation of my autonomy. What do you call it?"

"I call it love, goddammit, love!"

"In your mouth, they're the same thing."

"Kids! Kids! Let's keep this civil."

"Civil. All right, civil. I can do that." Jenny slapped Massey's hand so hard it stung. "Oh, look. You dropped your handheld." She stooped to retrieve it.

"What kind of idiot game are you playing now?" Massey went to take the device back but Jenny fended him off with her free arm. "I'd think that with an entire new life at stake, you'd take this a little more seriously."

"Where's the menu on this thing? Ah!" Jenny ran a finger down the screen and tapped twice.

"Hey!" Massey said.

"What's the matter? Can't move? Awwww, poor widdle baby."

"Goddammit, Jenny, this isn't funny. I don't know how you did this, but as soon as I can move again, I'm going to—"

She touched the screen, closed her eyes. "Sweet, sweet silence."

Long minutes passed. A gust of wind sent leaves raining down from the trees, making a soft sound when they hit the ground like playing cards falling on a felted poker table. In the stillness that followed, the air felt colder.

Unmuting Massey, Jenny said, "Okay, now you understand the rules. Keep a polite tongue in your mouth and you'll get all the answers you want."

"What's going on? I don't understand."

"You never told him, did you, Popsy?"

"I couldn't. You have no idea what George was like after the accident. Hysterical. Incapable of moving on. The grief counselor and I agreed that the best course of action was selective memory editing. We three had a little chat and he agreed to sign off on it."

"I'm not following any of this. Dad, what are you saying?"

"Son, Jenny wasn't alone in the car when she died."

Massey tried to clench his hands, but could not. "Oh. Right. Of course. Goddammit, I knew she was seeing somebody. You slut! I *knew* you were cheating on me."

"No. I wasn't. The other person in the car was you."

"Jenny, honey, are you sure you want to tell him this?"

"I do. Listen to me, George. We were arguing when you grabbed my arm and dragged me to the car. We were arguing when you hit the freeway at twice the speed limit. That was when I told you that anything was better than staying with you. You turned to look at me and your face—I can't describe it. It was a demon face. You said you'd see me dead before you let me go. Then you slammed the wheel over hard and drove us into that bridge embankment."

"I don't believe a word of this. It's not possible. I would never do anything to hurt you—never!"

"Popsy? You know more about this device than I do. Can you unblock his memories?"

The old man sighed. "Will do."

It was like God had reached down and flicked a switch in Massey's brain. He remembered everything. Every bitter word of the argument that had begun as a lunchtime discussion at the kitchen about where they should go on vacation. Something as trivial as that! But there had been a lot of resentment on both sides that had been building up over years of silence and once they started picking at them, everything came unraveled. Jenny had called him overbearing and controlling. He had called her a selfish bitch. Things went downhill from there. Until finally Massey knew he had to get out of the house and breathe some fresh air. But he couldn't bear to give Jenny the last word, so he had grabbed her wrist and pulled her after him. When he threw her into the car, he had no idea where he thought he was taking her. Nowhere, probably. Just away. And then . . .

He began to cry.

Jenny studied him without sympathy. "You get it now? You've been dead all along. You're just a ghost in a borrowed body, like me. Only I didn't want this and you did." She looked up at the moon. It made Massey's heart ache to see how its light silvered her face. She looked pure and ethereal. "I remember my relief when I realized I was about to die. Then my disappointment when the crash team brought me back. Death had solved all my problems. When they told me I got to choose whether to live or not, I was filled with joy. Yes, I said, death. Please."

"Oh God," Massey said. "Oh God, oh God." He took a deep breath. "This has got to be the worst moment in my life and I can't even find the words to . . . Dad! You've always got a quotation for everything. Help me out."

"Why, this is hell, nor am I out of it. Christopher Marlowe, *Doctor Faustus.*"

"Yeah, that's good. What you said. That'll do. Thanks." To Jenny, he said, "What now?"

"Now I'm going back to my nice, quiet grave. I'm afraid, however, that I can't leave you wandering about, coming up with who knows what goofball notions to lure me back to the land of the living. Your judgment's not very good. So I'm going to have to erase you from your artificial body."

"Baby girl, are you sure?" Massey's father asked.

"I am." With the old man's help, Jenny's thumb wandered over the handheld, tapping here and there. "Any last words?"

Forlorn, Massey shook his head.

Everything went black.

Afterward, Jenny transferred Massey's father into the male body and he transferred her back into her gravestone. "I'm sorry you had to be there when George died again," she said. "I wish he hadn't gotten you involved." Clouds covered the moon. The night was as dark as could be.

"Aw, I was never his father, after all. Not really. I'm just a self-aware program based on the old guy's personality."

"So. I'm settled. What are you going to do?"

"Well, I got this body, George's car, his house and property, his bank account . . . That'll do me until I get my business going."

"You're starting a business? What will you do?

"Take a long walk through every cemetery I can find, looking for those with unfinished business. Some of them I'll take into the body you didn't want and some into George's. I'll let them do whatever they want most. Get laid, eat a pineapple pizza, kill someone who deserves it. I'll give 'em a night to remember. For a price, of course. It's a rare corpse that doesn't have something stashed away where their heirs couldn't get their hands on it."

"You're a true humanitarian, Second Daddy."

"If by that you mean a scandalous old reprobate, then yes, I am. At any rate, I expect to have one hell of a lot of fun."

"Goodbye, then. Good luck. Come visit me sometime."

"Every Halloween," the old man said. "Like clockwork."

ABOUT THE AUTHOR

Michael Swanwick has been writing for over forty years, during which time he published eleven novels, over one hundred and fifty stories, and countless works of flash fiction. He has received the Nebula, Theodore Sturgeon, and World Fantasy Awards, as well as five Hugo Awards. He is best known for the Nebula-winning science fiction novel *Stations of the Tide,* and for his Iron Dragon fantasy trilogy.

Swanwick lives in Philadelphia with his wife, Marianne Porter.

Martial Arts and Fight Scenes in Zero-G: Research, Training, and Depictions in Film and Reality TV

D.A. XIAOLIN SPIRES

Space is not kind to the human body. Bodily fluids don't benefit from gravity to get pulled down to where they need to go so the face swells. Noses get blocked with congestion for similar reasons. The circulatory system is also affected, as blood volume may decrease and can cause dizziness. The heart, whose constant rigorous pumping so necessary on Earth, experiences a demotion to doing less work in zero-G, which could lead to its diminishment in size and potential decompensation. Ever been called small-hearted? Well, rather than a reference to cowardice or stinginess, in space, this could be a reference to a common physiological issue.

In general, bodily fluids get redistributed away from the lower extremities. Eventually, the muscles and bones in the lower part of the body (legs and hips) begin to give way, weakening. Not to mention, space sickness via disorientation, increased risk of cancer engendered by radiation exposure, cramped spaces, lack of nature sounds, and overall stress can compound these physiological issues, creating an amalgam of hurdles to wellbeing.

Given the dramatic and daunting changes the body undergoes in this environment, how does one effectively maneuver themselves especially in contexts of self-defense and bodily cultivation? Congested, nauseated, face-bloated, heart-diminished, muscle- and bone-weakened, how does one then use zero G to their full advantage to best an opponent? And how do works of science fiction portray martial arts and fight scenes in zero-G?

On Earth, we rely on that gravitational pull to deliver punches, kicks, strikes and holds. We can remain "rooted" and "draw energy from the ground." Our stances reflect our habituation to Earth's lovely gravitational field, the weighted feeling that being on home turf offers. Once we're floating about, how can we effectively outwit an opponent and deliver force by landing shots? On Earth, we have standup techniques, takedowns and ground techniques . . . in space, what do we have? Can you even "take someone down"? Does "down" even convey meaningful information and have the same connotations as on Earth?

There are many discussions of what is the 'best' martial art for particular situations. Rather than dive headlong into a fraught subject of superlatives in combat and self-defense, this article discusses both research of martial arts in zero-G (NASA experiments), as well as depictions of zero-G fight scenes in film and TV. Focusing away from the figurative comparison of each martial art's muscle and brawn as opposed to another in some cosmic scoresheet, this article will 'unearth' what is out there in terms of scientific research and fictional portrayal and 'probe' into the material.

For example, Adelina Bärligea,Kazunori Hase,andMakoto Yoshida all hope to"reveal insights into the feasibility of hand-to-hand combat in space" in the article "Simulation of Human Movement in Zero Gravity."

One of the researchers of the group practices karate and implements combat-related techniques inspired by the art with the aim to develop novel exercises for astronauts. The authors also employ recording and simulation technology such as depth- and orientation-sensing Microsoft's Azure Kinect DK and neuromusculoskeletal system-analyzing software Opensim.

The study concludes that while in zero-G, rotation is difficult and movement limited to bodily extremities. Keeping the rest of the body still seems to work better unless you grab onto other objects or people (i.e. "applying external contact forces" as the paper describes).

Various fight scenes in fictional zero-G involve projectile weapons or kicking off walls and objects. However, it may still be difficult to imagine a "static stance" while effectively pulling off karate-inspired techniques, as the paper describes. Movement of extremities, such as a punch, often involves twisting of the core, hips and legs in some way depending on the martial arts system. As the paper was published in *Sensors* journal, the focus may be on the technology of sensors within biomedical engineering contexts, with less focus on the applicable martial arts techniques described (were it, say, published in a martial arts magazine). It is interesting to note, though, that researchers are considering the mechanics of the body in combat and martial arts movements in relation to the future of space flight, medicine, and travel.

Similar movement in water or underwater provides a useful substitute to zero-G when training for spaceflight. Ever want to swim (or float for egress training) in the world's largest indoor pool? (At least that's what the NASA claims in its fact sheet from 2006. Things might be different now, in terms of pool superlatives on Earth.) Training to become an astronaut grants you access to the Neutral Buoyancy Laboratory (NBL) within the Sonny Carter Training Facility of the Johnson Space Center in Houston, Texas, which boasts of 6.2 million gallons of water. Of course, one must be a pretty decent candidate and compete in a rather intensive process to gain entry to the astronaut elite. One aspect of training is managing weightlessness and maneuvering through spacewalks, achieved through the neutral buoyancy ("equal tendency for an object to sink or float") according to a NASA fact sheet which simulates zero gravity.

It involves quite a few accoutrements: weights *and* flotation devices to achieve that state. Helmets on, suited up, gear sported, diver-assisted, the astronauts hover about in the water, bound to equipment, and attached to an umbilical cord of Nitrox breathing gas to reduce risk of experiencing the bends. (For the record, the umbilical cord is not present in spaceflight suits.)

There are also a few differences between neutral buoyancy and weightlessness: water drag is one of them; the other is that astronauts still perceive weight in their suits, even when bobbing along in the water. Yet, without traveling into outer space itself, this is probably the most Earthbound realistic scenario to train for spacewalks, availing ourselves of Earth's natural seemingly boundless resource: water.

If astronauts are capitalizing on the buoyancy of water to prepare for spacewalks, then how about martial artists who want to prep for zero-G? Yes, there are in fact, martial arts that specialize in techniques training underwater. Hawaii Zenyo JuJutsu Kai teaches Mizu Jitsu, in what they call an "Under Water Safety & Self-Defense Course." Their website asserts this course was developed by the suggestion of NASA, requesting for a "Weightless Environment Combat Course." While diving with the right credentials and training is quite safe and any encounters are mostly by accident rather than purposefully inflicted, this training covers emergencies not otherwise discussed in normal courses, including situations involving knives and spear guns.

Listed techniques involve body- and choke- escapes (grappling techniques), holds, sweeps, parries, nerve and pressure points, among others. One of the photos on the site depict one scuba diver manipulating the head of another (presumably a simulated opponent). The term zero gravity is not specifically mentioned on the website, but presumably the martial arts instructors are addressing weightlessness and approximation to zero gravity in their online reference to NASA.

While not specifically referencing approaching weightlessness or zero gravity simulation, other styles of martial arts include water training. Suijitsu or Suiei-jutsu is a form of Japanese combative swimming, harking back to the samurai era when bushi needed to deal with rivers and the surrounding ocean as part of combat.

In other martial arts, practitioners have employed water for training scenarios. The resistance provided by water makes shadowboxing and sprinting, and in general, water aerobics and water exercises, effective ways to sculpt muscles and train the body, while the buoyancy of water reduces stress on the joints and the muscular system. As an instructor, I've employed training in streams and bodies of water to provide different terrain experiences and movement challenges for martial arts practitioners. I have also tried boxing techniques while treading water, though none of these experiences have achieved the neutral buoyancy state mimicking weightlessness that the state-of-the-art space facility in Houston provides.

Another angle of analytical research in this vein of movement in liquid involves the feeling of the fetus in the womb, sensing a zero-G-adjacent impression involved in being suspended in amniotic fluid. Though one might protest that the fetus doesn't do martial arts, the fetus does begin to experiment with movement and locomotion, as it twitches, kicks, and switches positions in the womb. To be fair, microgravity rather than zero-G would be the better term for intrauterine fetal development conditions, according to Alexander Meigal and LiudmilaGerasimova-Meigal's article, "Cold for gravity, heat for microgravity: A critical analysis of the 'Baby Astronaut' concept" found in *Frontiers in Space Technologies*. Additionally, in an article in *Medical Hypotheses,* Slobodan Sekulic, Damir D Lukac, and Nada Naumovicargue that a fetus in earlier development, up to 21-22nd gestation week, experience "conditions similar to neutral floating."

Quickening, which involves fetal kicks and jabs, can be discerned as early as sixteen weeks, which means there is a period of crossover between the feeling of weightlessness and the fetus delivering forcible strikes with their feet, corroborating that the fetus is doing some, let's say, preliminary martial arts stunts in the near weightless womb.

Howard M Katz's article, "Escaping Gravity: Movie Magic and Dreams of Flying" ties the impulse or drive to move expansively as part of child development—"integral to ego development", linking physiological aims to volitional and psychological aims, to dreams of flying in fantasies and film. While Katz draws from Emanuel C. Wolff in psychoanalyzing flying, Wolff argues that the enjoyment of the sensation of flying is related to the experience of near zero-G in the womb, (i.e. "a vestige of the presymbiotic phase of development") whereas Katz thinks that the drive for flying as free movement is for its own right, as part of a child's development.

Katz's discussion also touches on the graceful, flying styles of the film *Crouching Tiger, Hidden Dragon* and associated wuxia cinema and Hong Kong action movies that precede it, with kicking and punching feats in apparent aerial weightlessness.

Admittedly, the article focuses more on child psychoanalysis rather than specific martial arts techniques, but does bring in portrayals of people fighting, flying, and gliding as related to the early drive for expansive movement as part of the analysis.

Speaking of movie magic, when the conversation about fight scenes in zero-G comes up, the prominent hallway fight scene of *Inception* arises in popular consciousness. And for good reason, if one looks at the behind-the-scenes technology that made it happen. A caveat: this is not a film about space, but about dreams, but zero-G still makes an appearance. In this film about stealing secrets from the subconscious, manipulating the mind, and cascading dreams within dreams, Joseph Gordon-Levitt as Arthur, fights his way through a hotel hallway against a "Projection"—a protection mechanism in the sleeper's subconscious mind. The hallway includes zero-G and shifting gravity as orientational frameworks to depict the shifting dreamscape. Innovative camerawork, tethered wires, and most notably the inclusion of three entire built sets of the hotel spaces were combined to create the effect. Strung from above, the actors sailed and floated through the vertical hallway for a zero-G effect. The rotating horizontal set allowed for shifts in gravity, so that Gordon-Levitt could jump from wall to ceiling to wall. The actors also floated, mounted, grappled, punched, and jumped about in a rotating hotel room set to simulate the effects of zero- and shifting gravity in fight scenes.

Gordon-Levitt revealed afterwards that he spoke to people who experienced zero-G to note that they were quite relaxed in their original environments but that while filming, he was the opposite since he had to simulate the look of zero-G while being quite subject to the effects of full gravity. If he didn't move in the direction of the rotation of the hallway or hotel room set, that could be a serious fall that could lead to a serious injury.

While the zero-G of space may be unkind to the human body, the gravity of Earth may be unkind to stunt people and actors performing high-flying feats, leaping to tackle an opponent, for example, as they must be particularly careful about the effect of impact.

One potential depiction of zero-G and fighting might be a mix of reality and TV fiction: reality TV. The premise of the possibly forthcoming sports competition show *Galactic Combat* is the culmination of the series: bringing the fight beyond Earth to zero-G space. Forty MMA fighters will train in zero-G conditions and thirty-two will be eliminated, resulting in eight competing Earthside. A rocket will take the two final contestants into orbit for 90 minutes so they can pummel each other in entertainment-making adrenaline, as they float and exchange blows in a specialized fighting capsule.

MMA fighter John Lewis has been promoting this concept and discusses its feasibility in terms of existing technology and in industry: space companies are already working on shooting films in space (i.e. the Russian film *The Challenge* directed by space-faring Klim Shipenko and the upcoming projected two hundred million dollar venture beyond our atmosphere with Tom Cruise and Space X).

Andrea Iervolino, who founded Space 11 Corp that is producing the *Galactic Combat* reality show, is discussing logistics with Elon Musk's SpaceX as well as the GAL Hassin International Center for Astronomical Sciences in Sicily. Space 11 has also partnered with the company Nanoracks in the hopes to fulfill a vision of a space station wholly dedicated to entertainment, including sporting events alongside musical concerts. The vision includes MMA-Zero gyms and a galaxy arena capable of seating six thousand enthused cosmic sports aficionados.

Having discussed research on martial arts-drawn movements in space, martial arts contending with approximations to zero-G or near-weightlessness, as well as film depictions of zero-G fight scenes employing martial arts techniques and potential future reality shows, there are numerous literary depictions which bring the floating fight to the textual page. In the next installment of this two-part series, we'll be looking at some of them including Fonda Lee's *Shadowboxer* and Orson Scott Card's *Ender's Game*. Stay tuned!

ABOUT THE AUTHOR

D.A. Xiaolin Spires steps into portals and reappears in sites such as NY, Hawai'i, various parts of Asia and elsewhere, with her keyboard appendage attached. Her work appears in publications such as *Clarkesworld, Analog,*

Strange Horizons, and anthologies of the strange and beautiful: *Make Shift, Deep Signal,* and *Sharp and Sugar Tooth.* Her works have been selected for The Year's Top Robot and AI Stories and The Year's Top Tales of Space and Time Stories, with poetry nominated for Rhysling, Best of the Net and Pushcart awards. She has a Ph.D. in socio-cultural anthropology and has conducted National Science Foundation-funded research. Her multifaceted writing reflects her interest in food systems, ecology, technology and society. She has mentored through SFWA and has taught academic and creative writing to students at the college level. She speaks multiple languages, savors durians, dekopon and rose-apples and teaches stick-fighting and weapons-based martial arts. Brush in hand, she also paints fantastical art in sumi ink, gouache, watercolor and acrylic. When she's not doing all these things, she is playing with meeples, cards and tiles, convening with good folk around a board game or RPG.

Teslapunk and Nerve Endings: A Conversation with Nalo Hopkinson

ARLEY SORG

Nalo Hopkinson was born in Kingston, Jamaica. She grew up there as well as Trinidad and Guyana, and spent some time in the US as a kid. Hopkinson moved with family to Toronto, Canada at age seventeen. She earned a Combined Honours B.A. from the York University in Toronto, majoring in Russian and minoring in French. She attended Clarion East (when it was held at Michigan State University) and later earned a Master's in Writing Popular Fiction from Seton Hill College, where James Morrow was her mentor. She moved to Riverside in 2011 to become a Professor of Creative Writing at the University of California, Riverside, where she was part of a faculty research cluster in science fiction.

Nalo Hopkinson was named a Grand Master by the Science Fiction and Fantasy Writers Association in 2021. She had a few stories come out in the 90s, such as "Riding the Red" in Ellen Datlow and Terri Windling's anthology *Black Swan, White Raven* (Avon Books, 1997) and "Tan-Tan and the Rolling Calf" in *Lady Churchill's Rosebud Wristlet* (Summer 1997). Debut novel *Brown Girl in the Ring* made a much larger splash. Published by Aspect/Warner in 1998, it received a number of awards nods, including finalist spots for the Crawford, Philip K. Dick, Aurora, and Otherwise Awards, and winning a Locus Award. It was likely the reason she won an Astounding Award for Best New Writer.

This was the beginning of a career of remarkable works, acknowledged in part by more awards nods and accolades than we can list here. Highlights include Sunburst and World Fantasy Award wins for collection *Skin Folk* (Aspect/Warner 2001), Sunburst and Aurora wins for *The New Moon's Arms* (Aspect/Warner 2007), an Andre Norton win for *Sister Mine* (Grand Central 2013), and a Sturgeon Award win for "Broad Dutty Water" (*The Magazine of Fantasy & Science Fiction*, Nov-Dec 2021).

In 2018 California State University Los Angeles gave Hopkinson the Octavia E. Butler Memorial Award, which celebrates an author whose writing exemplifies the spirit of Butler's work. That same year, Comic-Con International gave her the Inkpot Award, recognizing her achievements in science fiction. She has received honorary Doctor of Letters degrees from Anglia Ruskin University and the Ontario College of Art and Design University.

Nalo Hopkinson's body of work includes over forty short stories, several groundbreaking anthologies as editor or co-editor (beginning with 2_000's *Whispers from the Cotton Tree Root: Caribbean Fabulist Fiction*, published by Invisible Cities Press), three collections, and six novels.

Hopkinson is a professor in the School of Creative Writing at the University of British Columbia in Vancouver, Canada. Her latest books are her seventh novel: *Blackheart Man*, published in August of this year by Saga Press; and fourth collection *Jamaica Ginger and Other Concoctions*, just out last month from Tachyon.

What were the books, stories, or authors that were important to you when you were younger, the ones that influenced your writing or inspired you to write?

I'm sixty-three years old. I've been reading since I was three. My father was a poet, playwright, Shakespearean-trained actor and a high school English teacher. Before she retired, my mother was a library technician (NOT a librarian; there's a big difference). Our house was full of books and often, of the authors and artists who were my father's friends. My parents took us to readings and plays. How long would you like this answer to be? Actually, it's an impossible question to answer fully. I've forgotten and/or mentally rewritten lots of it. I read folktales and epic tales and some African fiction when I was young, started reading science fiction and fantasy as soon as I could have my own library card. Gravitated towards the New Wave writers, then the feminist wave of SF/F. Then I began to wonder where the Black writers were in the genre, and the other non-white writers.

At the time, in my twenties, the only Black writers in English I could discover were Samuel R. Delany, Octavia Butler, Tananarive Due, Steven Barnes in the U.S., and Charles Saunders in Canada. I eventually found Nisi Shawl, who'd just had their first short story published in *Asimov's*. So all of that was formative to me, from Chinua Achebe to William Shakespeare, from the folktales of many cultures to Homer's Iliad and Odyssey, from Ursula K. LeGuin to Samuel R. Delany. When I first began trying to write, maybe in my early thirties, I ended up in a workshop with a handful of other writers. Feminist author and editor Judith Merril met with us once, showed us how to run our own workshop, and sent us on our merry way. The bunch of us kept workshopping for a few years. Then there's all the inspiration I draw from other art forms; music, dance, poetry, visual arts, tv, film, etc.

You've been writing and publishing for a long time. What does it take to stay in the game for so long and sustain a career?

Every successful writer is going to have a different path to getting there. I have ADHD, fibromyalgia (ME), and I'm autistic. It's a miracle that I've completed anything I've written. I would read a lot of fiction—I don't do so as much nowadays—and I would read books about craft and tried to practice the things in them that resonated with me. I did research into the publishing side of the genre. Not hearsay, but library research and reading *Locus Magazine*. Once I started writing in my thirties, I wrote a lot. My workshop helped improve my skills. And I went for what educational opportunities I could afford. I was only able to afford Clarion through getting scholarships and a loan from a friend (thank you, Bob Boyczuk!)

My first novel was published as a result of entering and winning the Warner Aspect First Novel Contest. I'd been researching literary agents, and I began my novel publishing career with Donald Maass as my agent. In many ways, he's been a coach in the business side of publishing, as well as in how to craft novels. Each editor has taught me a little more about it. Other writers have been generous with their answers to my questions. And I kept writing and reading about writing craft, and submitting my short fiction to anthologies, and Don has continued pitching my work. My biggest challenge is persisting. With this brain, I'm not a "write every day" writer. I've had to find work to support me, because I don't produce regularly enough for my writing to do it.

This is your fourth collection, your second specifically with Tachyon. For you, what sets this one apart from previous collections?

I'd say this one has more stories that were first published in unconventional venues, such as to accompany arts exhibits. And I'm less concerned about what my writing might seem to be revealing about me. In any case, most people's guesses are inaccurate.

Thinking on the stories in this collection, do you see an underlying theme? Are there predominant concerns that these pieces come back to? Or are they all very different from each other thematically?

I think the underlying theme is me; my concerns, fascinations and obsessions. I'm obsessed with language, fascinated by and enthusiastic about vernacular speech, especially as a Caribbean person, enthusiastic about Anglo-Caribbean speech. I like re-imagining history from the perspective of the people who don't generally make it into the history books. I love the liminal in science fiction and fantasy. I'm interested in challenging people's biases (including my own) about race, gender, class, sex, sexuality, age. I enjoy using strong sensory metaphor to grab the reader by the nerve endings and pull them into my stories. I love the Caribbean region.

Are there one or two stories here you're particularly glad to see reach more or even just new readers? And what stands out for you about those pieces?

I confess I now have to go and find the table of contents for the forthcoming collection. As one publishes over and over, one begins to forget the specifics of each book. Lessee . . . "Child Moon" which I wrote at the beginning of COVID lockdown for *The Decameron Project*, an anthology inspired by COVID and *The Decameron*, a series of stories written by 14th Century author Boccaccio. The frame story of *The Decameron* is that some people are hiding from the 14th Century pandemic known as the Black Death, which killed about half of Europe at the time. As they shelter in place, hoping Death doesn't come calling, they tell each other stories.

I like "Child Moon" because of what I did with the worldbuilding and language, decentering the story from any one culture by using words that infer many. I know what I did, but I don't have a good way of explaining it. But I think it messes with reader expectations in lovely ways. Is it science fiction? Fantasy? Is it set on this Earth, or on another? Someone who heard me read it once asked me what happened to the baby in the story. I asked her which one. She replied, "the human one." I told her—spoiler—that they were both human. But as I think about it now, perhaps neither one of them is. Perhaps there are no humans in the story at all. Or perhaps every humanoid in it is in fact human.

Sometimes the works that artists love most are not necessarily the works that make the biggest splashes. Are there a couple of pieces here that were important or special to you, that you perhaps thought would resound more loudly in genre than they did when originally published?

I don't expect short stories to make a splash. Novels generally receive the lion's share of the attention. I do wish that more people grasped that the genre of "Jamaica Ginger", the eponymous short story co-written by me and Nisi Shawl, is not steampunk, but teslapunk. And not Tesla like the cars, but the 19th Century genius inventor Nikola Tesla. But maybe more people will know that now as a result of this interview. And perhaps "Inselberg", which you can read as science fiction or as a haunting.

Thinking back on the stories in this book, are there stories here that were more challenging to write, or perhaps more personal than usual?

"Repatriation" has personal significance to me. On the face of it, it's about two boyfriends taking a cruise ship back to their birthplace of

Jamaica. That story allowed me to make fun of some of the idiosyncrasies and excesses of cruise ship travel, and to find a bit of hope for dealing with the damage humans are doing to the oceans. As an island girl, I think about that damage a lot. They were all challenging to write, but "Propagation" brought me the closest to panic. I struggled and struggled with it, and was still writing it when I was flying to Vancouver to read it at TED. With about two hours to spare I confirmed that the science in it would not, could not work. But the conceit of it was integral to the story. I began to ask myself why I needed the story to play out that way. And I ended up with a piece that is part performance, part essay. It deconstructs itself and gets meta, and may not work on paper. But it worked as a reading, thank heaven.

Title Story "Jamaica Ginger" is unique in that it was coauthored with Nisi Shawl. Based on your bibliography, coauthoring is very rare for you. What made this story happen? What was the coauthoring process like?

Nisi may remember this more clearly than I do. I knew I wanted to write a story for the anthology *Stories for Chip*, which honors Samuel R. Delany. I even knew some of the elements of the story. But I was so tired! I think I contacted Nisi to ask whether they would like to co-write it with me. They said yes. Nisi has an essay at the beginning of *Jamaica Ginger and Other Concoctions* in which they describe the frustration of co-writing with me. I'd do a little bit then run out of steam and disappear. But their writing buoyed me up, and finally we pulled together a story of which I'm quite proud. Pullman porters and primitive Bluetooth, a clever young Black woman trying to escape her boss's clutches, and the real-world travesty that was Jamaica Ginger; a tonic which the American manufacturers diluted with what no-one knew at the time was a nerve toxin. It destroyed many lives. And a riff on *They Fly at Çiron*, one of Chip's lesser-known novels.

I used to balk at the idea of co-authoring. I wanted to keep my ideas to myself, and I feared collaboration would water them down. But then I was reading about the wonderful Leo and Diane Dillon. They were spouses and visual artists who created together. They did a lot of wonderful science fiction and illustrations, including the original cover of *Midnight Robber*, my second novel. Seems that when they first started out collaborating, they would each take one side of the canvas and paint in their own style; then they'd switch sides and work on each other's sketches until they achieved a synthesis of both their styles. That really caught my fancy. I began to understand that in a successful collaboration, you have to let go and open yourself to your collaborators' visions as well as your own. That's how you get something that's bigger than the sum of its parts. Your collaborators have to be people whose work you love, and that is definitely Nisi. It's the process I described to them, and they were down for each of us being able to edit and rewrite the other's parts. And it worked! I'm very proud of the result, and I hope Nisi is, too.

What, for you, is the heart of the title story – what is it about?

My stories are like squid, or Time Lords; you can assume they have more than one heart. Or maybe I just can't differentiate between a heart and other story organs once I've smooshed them together; they are all so interdependent. I can only speak for myself, not for Nisi. I've been interested for years in the African American history of the Pullman porters, how they deliberately hired newly emancipated Black people, how bad labor conditions led them to unionize, ultimately leading to the U.S. Civil Rights Movement. And I wonder what the world lost when Nikola Tesla was unable to get his amazing inventions to market, beat out by Edison.

Honestly, at first, I think I was mostly interested by automata, though none made their way into the story. But I guess that's all inspiration, not The Reason Why I (Co-)Wrote It. If I search for an answer, there's something I wanted to talk about that has to do with the ways in which systemic injustice affects Black lives and choices, including those of Plaquette, the young woman protagonist who's trying to find a way to support her aging parents that doesn't involve agreeing to become the mistress of her stingy, grasping white boss. In her time and place, that was a solution that would have raised no eyebrows. How do you escape an untenable life when there are no ways out? There. That's my answer today.

Do any of these stories have relationships to or connections with your recent novel Blackheart Man?

Actually, they don't. I tend to want to do something different in each piece I write.

What is important for readers to know about Blackheart Man?

It's a novel I was working on for about fifteen years, through many life challenges. I'm proud of having finally gotten it to the stage of being out in the world. I think it does some good stuff. My protagonist Veycosi is a scallywag, a privileged know-it-all whose saving grace is that he actually cares about other people. Sometimes he's likable. A lot of the time, he's exasperating.

Blackheart Man features multiple points of view, including Veycosi. What can you tell us about some of the perspectives we get to encounter in the book?

I'll try not to be too spoilerific. There's Androu, who left the island nation of Chynchin years before to escape prejudice there. Now he's back, bearing a grudge. There's Samra, a Chynchin woman from the same background as Androu, who also experiences systemic prejudice. She's one of Veycosi's love interests. There's the Blackheart Man, who's none too pleased about how life has buried him. And there may or may not be the occasional dip into the perspectives of deities and even an animal. Some reviewers have enjoyed the multiple perspectives; I was strategic about how often I used them. But for some, it's made their reading experience disjointed.

The Publishers Weekly review says "Hopkinson's worldbuilding astonishes" and the Locus review describes Chynchin as "textured and believable". In terms of craft, what is the key to developing a fantasy narrative with textured, believable, and astonishing worldbuilding?

I love it that they both praised my worldbuilding! In first draft, I tend to do it on the fly, discovering the world as I draft the story. Then I'll realize I need to know more about the world of the story, so I'll make some notes, typically supported by research. I'll go back and forth like that in subsequent drafts. Ultimately, I will know more about the world than makes it into the story. I try to put in elements of worldbuilding only insofar as the characters have contact with those details. "Contact" can be physical, or it can be intangible, such as a social expectation. Limiting my worldbuilding on the page that way helps to keep the incidence of expository lumps low and brief. I mean, sometimes you need that kind of exposition, but I find that for me, it's usually best when it happens to get in and out quickly, hopefully before the reader gets pulled too far out of the story by explanatory chunks. I'm trying to intrigue the reader, to get them to join me in the imaginative game of creating the world of the story. Sometimes it doesn't even matter whether what they imagine from my clues is a bit different than what I intend.

I also use strong metaphors and imagery for physical sensation and movement. Research has told us that when we read uninflected description ("the sun came up"), not much happens for us. But use strong metaphor and imagery for sensation ("the morning sun leapt, singing, into the Saturday sky,") and our nerve endings associated with those sensations actually fire. In other words, we're now living in the description. When you write that way, you're building a Holodeck world for your readers to wander around in. As Ed Finn describes fiction as an "empathy engine." I think that in spec fic, we're trying to get our readers to identify with experiences that can't or haven't happened. That's part of the challenge and the play of writing it.

Is there anything else you'd like readers to know about either or both of these books, Jamaica Ginger and/or Blackheart Man?

Not really. It's been a while, and I'm so happy to have new books of mine out in the world again!

What else do you have going on, in the works, or coming up that you'd like readers to know about?

There will be a graphic novel coming from Abrams in due course; a collaboration I'm doing with the brilliant artists Steve Bissette (*Saga of the Swamp Thing*), and John Jennings (*Blue Hand Mojo*). The three of us devised the story together, and I wrote the script. It's called *Night Comes Walking*, and the genre is horror, based on two historical figures. Writer/sociologist/hoodooist Zora Neale Hurston (*Their Eyes Were Watching God*) and decorated former military man Eugene Bullard (first African American fighter pilot) go on a road trip to discover who's using poisonous snakes to launch deadly supernatural attacks on B&Bs along the routes of *The Green Book for Negro Travellers*. John and Steve, both lovely men, have some seriously creepy imaginations, and it was a blast combining mine with theirs.

ABOUT THE AUTHOR

Arley Sorg is an associate agent at kt literary. He is a two-time World Fantasy Award Finalist and a two-time Locus Award Finalist for his work as co-Editor-in-Chief at *Fantasy Magazine*. Arley is also a SFWA Solstice Award Recipient, a Space Cowboy Award Recipient, and a finalist for two Ignyte Awards. Arley is senior editor at *Locus*, associate editor at both *Lightspeed* & *Nightmare*, a columnist for *The Magazine of Fantasy and Science Fiction* and an interviewer for *Clarkesworld*. He is a guest critiquer for the 2023 Odyssey Workshop, and is the week five instructor for the 2023 6-week Clarion West Workshop, among other teaching and speaking engagements.

Cyberpunk Economics: A Conversation with Eliane Boey

ARLEY SORG

Eliane Boey was born and raised in Singapore. She had wanted to study history but her parents were more . . . pragmatic: "I had the privilege of a university degree where my parents didn't, so I was expected treat uni as preparation for a 'good job.' Undergrad business school at Singapore Management was so that they could sleep at night, and grad school was for me." Boey studied Philosophy at the University of St Andrews, and Interdisciplinary Humanities at New York University, including healthy doses of political theory and urban studies. "I was relieved when the Interdisciplinary Program at NYU 'rehabilitated' me back into the Arts." During one of the lockdowns in Singapore, she did an online writing workshop with Erin Kelly and Sarah Hilary, focusing on Crime and Thriller Writing—conducted for Curtis Brown. "It was such a lifesaver. I was writing an historical/dual timeline thriller at the time, and I lived in the course chat forums."

Boey has worked front-of-house for a theatre company, for a while was taking night classes in fashion design, took a pattern drafting course at a dressmaking studio, and at one point, she staged a haute cuisine restaurant. For her day job she works with dry bulk ships and port logistics. "It's taken me to mines, company towns, and port complexes around the world, and onboard some of the biggest vessels at sea . . . I don't have a science background, so I take what I know about ships and slap them on spacecraft. Make it work. My novella 'Carrier' has a little bit of an adventure in maritime law and creative approaches to vessel stability that I still hope my old colleagues will never pick up."

Eliane Boey hit the fiction scene with "The Quiet Tailor" in *Mekong Review* (February 2022), followed by "Ghost Crab" in *The Penn Review* (#71, Spring, June 2022). Her first genre magazine appearance came next, with "The Forgotten" in the July 2022 *Clarkesworld*. Her work continued to appear in a range of magazines, including "Hunger" in *Weird Horror #6* in 2023 and "Sea Walkers" in *Solarpunk #16* in 2024.

Dark Matter INK published *Other Minds* in September 2023, "a duology of cyberpunk and space horror novellas." Her latest is debut novel *Club Contango*, coming out December 3, 2024 with Dark Matter INK.

What has your relationship to reading and writing been like over the years?

I always loved reading fiction. Funny thing is I always thought I was a reader, not a writer, as though those had to be different things. When I wrote short stories and essays for school, I was hyper critical of my own work, and so I never went through that writer's rite of passage (that I believe so many have?) of making a stapled/ring-bound handwritten first novel in school. In many ways, I've still never shaken off that rapid imposter syndrome.

When I eventually gave writing fiction a chance, it was 2019, I was in a new (dream) job, I'd recently had my kid, then the company went belly up, the floor hit the ceiling and I thought, I suppose I don't think I have anything to lose by trying to write *now*.

I'm a millennial, but I had a very gen-X upbringing, and I spent a lot of my time after school sitting on the wall-to-wall carpet of the second-hand bookstore in the tired old neighborhood shopping center across our flat, reading. And then going to the food court to buy my meal and continue reading. Then going home to read under my table in semi darkness. (Kids, don't do this. I have terrible eyesight.) Anyway, I'm glad I stopped thinking within those limits, and started writing.

I guess when I look back now, I spent a lot of time wrestling with my highly practical life, and trying to get back to writing. From transitioning from business school to grad school in philosophy—I quit my first corporate job to go back to school again and that made sense to absolutely no one—to trying other creative hobbies, and now, taking the time to pause and write. I feel I've always been trying to find my way back to writing, and I'm glad I finally gave myself a chance to.

Who were the authors or what are the works that inspired you when you were younger, and who are the authors or what are the works that inspire you lately?

I did not grow up on SFF. As a child I read and loved Lloyd Alexander, C.S. Lewis, Mervyn Peake, and Michael Crichton. But I mostly grew up on older classics, spy thrillers, mystery, and 1990s legal thrillers, because that was what was available at the second-hand bookstore near my parents' flat.

The first SFF books I read as an adult were Samit Basu's *The City Inside* and Edward Ashton's *Mickey7*, followed by Ken Liu's Dandelion Dynasty. Since then, I've likewise been inspired by the works of N.K. Jemisin, Aliette de Bodard, and Silvia Moreno-Garcia. I also enjoy reading Dennis Lehane and S.A. Cosby. And I sometimes reread the work of Patricia Highsmith and John le Carré. And while we're on crime, 1990s Hong Kong cinema has also been something of an influence on my writing.

How has your publishing journey been so far, including getting books Other Minds and Club Contango published? Were there struggles in terms of getting established, or did you sell short fiction immediately, and find that subsequently, everything would just fall into place?

Publishing struggles come in as many variants as there are writers, don't they?

I think I've sold a little over half of the short stories that I wrote since my first story publication. Funny enough, once I started writing novellas, every idea I had came with tails and necks that stretched out into long form, and I haven't written any short fiction this year. I promised myself I'd get back to it as soon as I finish the novel I'm working on now. So she said.

The biggest struggle for me is trying to do what I can to market my books, while living outside the publishing epicenter. I hope to travel for writer conferences and book events soon, and I am grateful to all the editors who have taken a chance on me, and those hopefully to come. But it's important to acknowledge that location does affect ability to find and connect with booksellers and readers.

Club Contango is your debut novel, but you have been selling short fiction for a couple of years now, and your previous book, Other Minds, features two novellas. Has writing at shorter lengths helped to prepare you for novel-length work? Are there relationships within the practice of writing at different lengths?

I'd write novellas exclusively if I could, although I feel "longform" somewhere between 30k and 60k is about as much as I usually need. I don't have a lot of short fiction behind me, but what I do have has taught me to edit myself ruthlessly. And so far, the way I approach novels is by writing a mostly complete novella first. Then I go back, and look for branches that can be developed, subplots worth expanding, and pockets where the story has space to grow. I think writing that way helps keep my novels tight and coherent.

Thinking about your body of work to-date, do you feel like there are themes, ideas, or vibes that you tend to come back to often? Or do you feel like each piece is completely different from the next?

I write about mummy/daddy/mentor issues in space, with economics. Seriously now. One theme that keeps coming back is rebuilding yourself; finding and grounding and loving yourself as you are, and often while having to care for others. I center imperfect, reluctant, and often insecure protagonists who are strong because they have no choice but to be. Who can't easily compartmentalize or discard the different things that they are at once, or stop the world for an adventure. Another theme is loneliness in a crowd, and the feeling of being left behind. That is what I keep coming home to.

My short stories have been more varied, because I tend to use them to experiment. I've written weird horror too, although I don't think that's my strength.

If readers unfamiliar with your writing were to look up just one of your shorter works, what would you want them to read, and why?

I'd love for more people to read "Saturation", in *Dark Matter* #18. That story's almost a novelette, and it's subtler than my other work and has a dreamier voice than my novellas and *Club Contango*, but it carries a number of themes regularly cooking in my head. It's sort of *A Doll's House* meets *Gattaca*, and I had a great time writing it.

You've described Club Contango as "SF Noir" or "Cyberpunk Noir"—what does "Noir" mean for you and how does this book embody noir?

I acknowledge that there are multiple ways of writing and reading the genre(s) that make sense for different people. For me, noir and cyberpunk have displacement, alienation and distrust in institutions in common.

If I'm not mistaken, noir found its voice in the inter-world world war period. We meet the imperfect, conflicted urban protagonist, who loves their city, evidenced in a strong anchoring of place. Yet the city doesn't offer much comfort back, the familiar spaces beckon but seem haunted by unease and foreboding, and consequently the noir protagonist is a lone figure who belongs and is displaced at the same time.

Noir can feel hyper-real from the grit and smoke, the same way that cyberpunk can fixate on tech-entrenched life and loneliness. But what the characters are really doing is grasping for new anchors and new meaning in a world that is leaving them behind. So, cyberpunk, like the noir genre, deals in lost illusions and broken promises of the future, hence the loneliness, and distrust. And the characters who cut themselves off and strike out alone for the indispensable smoky alley, or sheeting rain ricocheting off neon-reflecting puddles, to reclaim what it means to be human.

That said, what I hope to achieve with my cyberpunk to is bring the element of hope through community and friendship into it. So yes, I've jokingly called *Club Contango* an "uplifting" book, just not the sort you'd expect.

Paul McAuley, in his review of Other Minds for IZ Digital, described the book as a "richly envisioned noir mystery . . . " In terms of craft, what do you feel is the key to writing fiction which is "richly envisioned"?

And I'm so thrilled he thought so! *Other Minds* contains the novellas "Signal\Tracer" and "Carrier". Both have very different settings across a shared world. The former takes place in a sort of high-functioning urban dystopia, and the latter almost entirely on a spacecraft. When I wrote those novellas, I tried to make the setting as much a character as the protagonists themselves.

Of the components of a story, I find scene descriptions the hardest to write. When I write, I begin with dialogue, external and internal, and I leave world descriptions for later drafts. I'll describe the setting if it means something or does something for the characters and their story. I suppose that's my approach to world-building.

Club Contango features single mom Connie Lam as protagonist. What do you love most about this character, and what were some of the challenges in writing her?

(CW: depression) Connie Lam is depressed, overworked, and has nothing left for herself. She tries to keep it together, but she's pulling at strings. Everyone wants a piece of her for themselves. To her aging parents back on Earth, she's a bridge to the changing world; to her boss/mentor she's the earnest and selfless young acolyte; to her friends, she's a mate who's always up for a new scheme. On top of that, she tries to hold a fount of time and patience for her kid. Connie feels she's failed on all these fronts. And she's also a visa over-stayer. The murder, the space gangsters, the replicants, and the clubs and wild living on Freeport Station keep the story a fun and darkly humorous read, but this is Connie's story.

All that is to say that I love Connie's ability to scrape the dry well feeling like she's left behind in her own life, and laugh at herself while doing it. Until she can't.

What was the initial inspiration for Club Contango, and how did the story change or develop across drafts and edits?

Club Contango is a number of firsts for me. It was the fastest novel I wrote to completion. In some ways it's hard to trace my exact inspiration for it, because it just came together as the freezer-clearing leftover stew of my head. But it began with my short story "Contango" (*Dark Matter* #16). I'd been wanting to write a story about trading the future for a little while.

By the way, if you've read that short story, both protagonists are not the same person. "Contango" predates *Club Contango* in my story world, and there's a bit of connecting lore you'll just have to read the novel to find out!

Anyway, I finished writing "Contango" the short, but I wanted to keep writing about that fraying mum plugging away at work she despised, for people she shouldn't trust with her wallet, let alone her kid's life, but had no other choice. And the films *Boiler Room* and *Fight Club* were really sitting on my head during that time. As well as *Sorrow and Bliss* by Meg Mason, which deals with depression with a big spoonful of dark humor. So, I wrote a novella version of *Club Contango* and pitched it to Rob at Dark Matter INK. When he bought it, I expanded it into a novel in about three months. It was the first work I wrote without a plan. All I knew was that I cared fiercely about Connie Lam, and I wanted to give her a story.

In terms of science fiction, this book has an international space city, AI, and much more. If you can share some things without spoiling the experience of the read too much, what are some of your favorite science fictional aspects, ideas, or elements of this book?

If science fiction turns on a speculative "scientific" element that changes everything in that world, then I tend to describe the SF qualities in my work as being, actually, economics. Yes, there are all those elements you mentioned, and some of them are just aesthetics, good food, and vibes—because I try to live a little—but it's the economic patterns and structural rules, and the ground-level reactions to them, that drive these elements of the world and make it what it is. Xi and Wei in "Signal\Tracer" wouldn't be best friends on opposite sides of a virtual nostalgic playground if it weren't for a flawed execution of universal income and rigid definitions of division of labor.* Connie wouldn't be left with no spoons and terrible choices if it weren't for an unforgiving work skills and immigration vetting system on Freeport.

*(When I wrote "The Forgotten", which was the *Clarkesworld* story that "Signal\Tracer" came to be based on, I didn't set out to write science fiction, but a mystery.)

What is the heart of Club Contango for you? What is this book about for you?

When the lights are turned on over the dance floor and the jokes are forgotten, I hope *Club Contango* will be remembered as a book about reaching in for your best self, but also accepting what you are while you get there. I hope it finds the people who need it.

What else are you working on? What do you have out or coming up that you'd like Clarkesworld readers to know about?

I have another space-set thriller, completed, that I hope will get picked up soon. If you've read one of my shorter stories, "Constant Dawn" in *Galaxy*, that's a taste of what's coming. And I'm currently working on an urban fantasy that's knocking me out of my head. But until those become reality, please preorder *Club Contango*!

ABOUT THE AUTHOR

Arley Sorg is an associate agent at kt literary. He is a two-time World Fantasy Award Finalist and a two-time Locus Award Finalist for his work as co-Editor-in-Chief at *Fantasy Magazine*. Arley is also a SFWA Solstice Award Recipient, a Space Cowboy Award Recipient, and a finalist for two Ignyte Awards. Arley is senior editor at *Locus*, associate editor at both *Lightspeed* & *Nightmare*, a columnist for *The Magazine of Fantasy and Science Fiction* and an interviewer for *Clarkesworld*. He is a guest critiquer for the 2023 Odyssey Workshop, and is the week five instructor for the 2023 6-week Clarion West Workshop, among other teaching and speaking engagements.

Editor's Desk: I Think We Can, I Think We Can

NEIL CLARKE

At the World Fantasy Convention last month, Guest of Honor and *Beneath Ceaseless Skies* editor, Scott Andrews gave a speech that echoed a sentiment I've expressed in various posts, panels, and Best Science Fiction of the Year introductions: that the field needs to make paying editors (and the rest of the staff) a priority. Such proclamations are usually met with a sheepish silence, particularly when you mention that it presents a financial barrier that limits who can participate in the field.

It's often bemoaned that you "can't make a living from short fiction." I'm not convinced that is true. While the overall culture around short fiction shifted to an expectation of it being free, that doesn't mean that it has no value or that no one can afford it. It's just something most people don't give a second thought to until they have to. Sentiments like Scott's play a role in keeping the importance of paying people involved in short fiction in the public eye. You never know what will trigger a change, but we know that silence won't. Is it too much to hope that someday people will champion paying staff in the same way they did for fast food workers?

One of the reasons that many of us place short fiction online for free is to remove financial and access issues that might otherwise prevent someone from engaging with it. It's part marketing, part altruism. It doesn't matter if the magazine is for-profit or a non-profit, we all want to see short fiction grow in popularity. We recognize its important place in the SF/F ecosystem as a gateway for new voices, ideas, and techniques. The importance of it being a career was somehow lost in the mix, but even more so for staff than authors.

SFWA (the Science Fiction and Fantasy Writers Association) has historically done a good job advocating for author pay. (Changes in membership criteria have removed the teeth from much of their advocacy in this respect, so I have concerns about their continued influence on this point.) The current accepted minimum standard is only eight cents per word. There's a large number of publications that pay less because they simply can't pay that much and a significant number of them that pay those rates, only are able to do so by cutting corners elsewhere. Most commonly, it comes at the expense of making staff positions unpaid or token-pay jobs. This is a mistake I will freely admit to having made myself in the early days of *Clarkesworld*. We have, however, made redressing the mistakes of our past a priority and have successfully moved that needle a bit.

A common criticism of the SFWA rate is that it has not kept pace with inflation. In a *Forbe*'s article about *Astounding* (a book sharing the name of the magazine edited by John W. Campbell, Jr.), Alec Nevala-Lee noted that "Before World War II, the rate in *Astounding* for a popular author like [L. Ron] Hubbard came to a penny and a half per word" which calculated for inflation would come to around thirty-three cents per word today.

That's an oversimplification. It fails to take into consideration decreases in total paid circulations–which have fallen sharply since 1938–and increases in cover prices. Those alone would suggest a modern pay rate of closer to twelve cents per word for the same publication and much less for almost everyone else. That too, leaves out complicating factors. The cost of printing and shipping, for example, have increased at a rate outpacing inflation in recent years. In the end, eight-to-ten cents per word might not be terribly unreasonable from a strictly mathematical perspective and that would be the top end.

[It's interesting to note that when these conversations do come up, no one ever points out that if you were an editor in 1938, you were paid. If you weren't, you expected to be and your boss was probably a crook. It wasn't expected that you'd keep working for nothing.]

All things considered, we probably shouldn't be looking at any math based on 1938 as a guiding light for modern-day authors or staff. The industry has changed considerably since then. Massive declines in readership, distribution collapses, the rise of digital, an explosion in the number of new markets, and so much more have rewritten what the field is today. The only constant is that paid readership makes it all possible. Advertising is virtually non-existent, grants are rare, and sponsorship, unreliable. It's why the termination of the Amazon subscription was such a big deal. It dealt a sharp blow to our most financially-successful publications and the uncertainty it caused still ripples outward.

While we focused on surviving that transition, I temporarily suspended all planned pay increases and adjustments. When we finally managed to rebuild our post-Amazon subscriber base this past August, it was the first thing we restarted. In my November 2021 editorial, I said:

> "Last month, we increased our pay rate for authors/translators from ten to twelve cents/word. Since they were paid better than everyone else from the start, each cycle on the spreadsheet ends with a boost to author pay. This increase signals the completion of one major round of pay adjustments. Do I consider twelve cents/word to be professional? Hell no. It's just a step and there's many cycles left to go. It's a long spreadsheet."

I am proud to say that thanks to our readers, we are on the cusp of completing the next cycle. Assuming the subscription numbers hold, we are on course to increase our author and translator pay rates to fourteen cents per word! This is an extraordinarily good sign for the entire team and something we are very grateful to our readers for helping us accomplish. The job is far from complete, but each milestone means a lot and sends a message that progress can be made.

Interestingly, if we were using the inflation/paid circulation/cover price formula that I used for *Astounding*, *Clarkesworld*'s rate would be less than a penny per-word. Our staff would be paid a little better, but we see our authors as part of the current mess, just like the rest of us. Here, we all move forward as one using a formula for 2024, not 1938.

Thank you all for your continued support and encouragement, particularly those of you who have helped spread the word in the last year.

ABOUT THE AUTHOR

Neil Clarke is the editor of *Clarkesworld Magazine, Forever Magazine,* and several anthologies, including the Best Science Fiction of the Year series. He is a three-time winner of the Hugo Award for Best Editor Short Form, the 2024 winner of the Locus Award for Best Editor, a four-time winner of the Chesley Award for Best Art Director, and a recipient of the Kate Wilhelm Solstice Award. His next anthology, *Best Science Fiction of the Year: Volume 8*, was published by Night Shade Books in September. He currently lives in NJ with his wife and two sons.

The Citizen of Ethos

COVER ART BY PABLO MUNOZ GOMEZ

ABOUT THE ARTIST

Pablo Munoz Gomez is a concept and character artist, as well as founder of the websites ZBrushGuides and 3Dconceptartist. His work involves visual development and sculpting in both 3D and traditional media. His work has been published in various books such as *ZBrush Characters and Creatures, Sculpting from the Imagination in ZBrush*, and the *Artist Guide to the Anatomy of the Human Head*, as well as industry media & magazines.

Printed in the USA
CPSIA information can be obtained
at www.ICGtesting.com
CBHW020548071124
16994CB00005B/22

9 781642 361759